"Excuse me, ladies, I'm Jack Germaine,"

a nicely dressed older man said, tapping Marina on the shoulder. "Call me Jack."

"Yeah?" Marina said over the music, which had started up again.

"You two are fabulous dancers!" he yelled.

"Thanks!" Sam said. She never got tired of hearing it.

"I really mean it," Jack continued. "You're both terrific. Outstanding!"

Sam smiled some more, but she thought the guy was laying it on a little thick.

"Well, excuse us!" Marina yelled so Jack could hear her. She grabbed Sam's arm and started to move away.

"Just one thing," Jack said, stopping them. "How would you both like jobs as professional dancers?"

Sunset Heat

CHERIE BENNETT

Virgin

First published in Great Britain in 1994 by
Virgin Books
an imprint of Virgin Publishing Ltd
332 Ladbroke Grove
London W10 5AH

First published in the USA in July 1991 by
The Berkley Publishing Group
published by arrangement with
General Licensing Company, Inc.

Printed and bound by
Cox & Wyman Ltd, Reading, Berks

ISBN 0 863 69806 9

A NOTE FOR BRITISH READERS FROM
THE PUBLISHERS

This story is set in the United States of America and has been
written in American English. We feel that the American
spelling, grammar and vocabulary that Cherie Bennett uses in
her writing are an important part of the story, and we haven't
changed anything that was in the original American edition.
Therefore, be warned: you will find in this book words,
phrases and spellings that are not usual, and sometimes
downright incorrect, in British English.

Now and forever, for Jeff

AUTHOR'S NOTE: The author wishes to thank family therapist Irma Gottesfeld, M.S.W., of Englewood, New Jersey, for information about counseling an adult adopted child and her parents.

ONE

"Hey, Sunset Island, I'm baaaaaack!" Samantha Bridges screamed into the wind. She was on the top deck of the ferry, and she could just make out the dock in the distance. As the wind whipped her long red curls into her eyes and the salt spray from the water tickled her face, a feeling of unbelievable happiness came over her. She threw out her arms to embrace all the possibilities that awaited her—adventure, romance, maybe even love. *Back to my favorite spot on earth with my two best friends and a few hundred gorgeous guys*, she sighed to herself. *Sheer bliss.*

Sam closed her eyes and let the sun warm her face as she thought back on the past year of her life. She'd come to Sunset Island the previous summer to be an au pair for the Jacobses, right after she'd graduated from high school in Junction, Kansas. Sam wrinkled her nose at the memory of that—Kansas was her idea of purgatory.

It had been Sam's job to care for Dan Jacobs's identical twin daughters, Allie and Becky, who had been thirteen years old at that time. She was basically a live-in nanny. But Allie and Becky had turned out to be quite the handful. They were extremely precocious—to put it mildly. One of their rules had been never to date a guy *under* the age of sixteen.

Fortunately, Sam had became fast friends with two other girls she had met at the National Au Pair Society convention in New York. Although Carrie Alden and Emma Cresswell were as different from Sam (and from each other) as they could possibly be, the three of them had formed a bond that was unshakable. It was true that sometimes Sam felt envious of Emma's money, and teased her about it, and sometimes the fact that Carrie did everything so perfectly and was so *good* made Sam crazy, but still Carrie and Emma had become the two best friends she'd ever had.

The friendship had lasted, too. At the end of the summer Emma had begun her freshman year at snooty Goucher College in

Maryland, Carrie had gone away to Yale in Connecticut, and Sam had started at Kansas State on a dance scholarship. They had stayed in touch through letters and phone calls—although Sam had to admit that both Carrie and Emma were better about it than she was.

Sam opened her eyes. The ferry was about to dock. A smile played around her lips as she thought of how much she and Emma and Carrie had already been through together.

They'd had two big reunions since the previous summer. When Sam had dropped out of college to be a dancer at Disney World in Orlando, Florida, Emma and Carrie had come down for a Christmas reunion. And at spring break, Emma had picked up Sam in her new convertible and they'd driven up the coast, scooping up Carrie from Yale on the way. They'd ended up at a big party right here on the island. Sam's smile faded when she remembered how the party had ended in disaster.

But this summer they were older and wiser—not too old, however, to have a wild and crazy summer. Sam would see to that.

"Sam! Hi! Great to see you!" Dan Jacobs called as she walked off the ferry.

Sam looked up, and couldn't believe what she saw. *Is this really Mr. Jacobs?* she thought, incredulous, as he pumped her hand enthusiastically. Conservative Mr. Jacobs, whom she'd never been able to bring herself to call Dan? The previous summer, his hair had been almost militarily short, and his wardrobe had consisted of the world's nerdiest baggy pants and wash-and-wear button-down shirts—in other words, outfits that had done little to flatter his couch-potato body. Now, standing there before her was an attractive man in his late thirties with slicked-back hair that reached his collar in the back, faded jeans, and a torso-fitting T-shirt that showed off serious muscle definition.

"Mr. Jacobs?" Sam said. "You look . . . you look . . ."

"He looks great, doesn't he?" piped up a familiar voice from behind her. Sam turned around, and Becky Jacobs threw herself into Sam's arms. At least Sam thought it was Becky. The only way she could tell the twins apart was by remembering that Allie had a beauty mark above her mouth. Becky was about two inches taller than she had been the previous summer, her hair was long and wild-looking, she had on too much makeup,

4

and she was dressed in a tiny miniskirt and a revealing halter top.

"Yep, I'm Becky," Becky said, reading Sam's thoughts. "Wow, I'm so glad to see you! This is way cool!"

Sam was gratified at Becky's enthusiasm. The truth of the matter was that she and the twins hadn't always gotten along swimmingly the previous summer. In fact, Sam had almost immediately dubbed the twins "the monsters."

"Where's Allie?" Sam asked.

"She's getting a Coke," Becky said. "And guess what? It isn't hard to tell us apart anymore."

"Why is that?" Sam asked. The answer to her question became apparent as Allie walked toward her from the Coke machine.

"Hello, Samantha," came a quiet, well modulated voice.

"Allie?" Sam asked. *This is just too weird*, she thought. Allie had short, straight hair and she wore no makeup at all. Her skirt hung below her knees, and she had on a Peter Pan–collared white shirt that was buttoned up all the way.

"Yes, it's me," Allie said in that same bizarre voice. "We're so happy to have you join us this summer."

Sam tried to keep a normal look on her face because it seemed like Allie was serious. "Oh, yeah. Me, too," she said.

"Come on, the car's right over here," Mr. Jacobs said, easily lifting Sam's two huge suitcases.

"Well, there've been some . . . changes!" Sam said in what she hoped was a cheerful voice as Mr. Jacobs headed the car down Beachfront Street.

"Well, I started taking my health seriously," Dan Jacobs said as he turned the corner. "I joined a gym and took off twenty pounds!"

"That's fabulous!" Sam said.

"Yeah, and as soon as he did he dropped Stephanie," Becky said from the back seat. "Really bogus move, if you ask me."

Stephanie was Mr. Jacobs's girlfriend from the previous summer. Sam was surprised they'd broken up—at the time, they had been practically engaged.

"That's not why we broke up," Mr. Jacobs corrected his daughter. "I've told you that before."

"Well, it sucks, if you ask me," Becky mumbled.

"Please, Becky, they weren't on the same spiritual plane," Allie chided her sister.

Becky caught Sam's eye in the front seat. "Has she changed, or what?"

"I no longer need to act like a child, that's all," Allie said, staring out the window. "I'll pray for you."

Becky leaned closer to Sam. "It's very weird, I'm telling you. She's decided to become a nun."

"A *nun?*" Sam repeated. "Last year she was trying to skip her teen years and move right on to her wild twenties."

Becky shrugged. "Go figure. I tried to tell her she can't become a nun. We're Jewish. But she won't listen."

"Home, safe and sound!" Dan Jacobs said cheerily as he pulled the car into the driveway.

He carried Sam's suitcases up to her room. "I'll just let you get settled in, and we'll talk at dinner, okay?" Mr. Jacobs asked.

"Fine. Thanks, Mr. Jacobs," Sam said.

"Hey, really, this summer you have to call me Dan," Mr. Jacobs said. "I insist."

"Okay, Dan," Sam answered. It sounded very strange.

"Good. See you in a few!"

Sam sat down on her bed. She looked around at the familiar room. It seemed like

7

home. How many times had she combed her hair in that mirror, or lain in bed trying to figure out her life? Of course, this was probably the neatest it would be for the duration of the summer, but time was short and there were more important things to think about. Here she was, back again. It felt great.

Sam kicked off her trademark red cowboy boots and wiggled her toes into the thick carpet, falling back on the bed. Just then Becky stuck her head around the door.

"Can I come in?"

"Sure," said Sam. This was definitely an improvement. The old Becky would have simply entered without knocking.

"Listen, like I said, I'm glad you're here and everything," Becky said, running one finger along the dresser. "But you're not gonna really, like, *babysit* us, are you?"

"No," Sam assured her. "Your dad and I discussed it. I'll be kind of a companion. A big sister, sort of."

"One sister is enough, thank you," Becky said, rolling her eyes.

"Okay, how about older friend, then?" Sam suggested. "I mean, you guys can't drive yet, so I'll take you to the club, stuff like that."

"Well, all right," Becky said, "but you understand that I would die if anyone thought we had a babysitter again this summer. I'll just tell my friends you're visiting me, okay?"

"Fine with me," Sam said. "But I've still got to work the details out with your dad."

"If you can ever find him," Becky said. "Now that he's great-looking he thinks he's Joe Stud. He goes out all the time."

"Oh," Sam answered in a pleasant voice. This was not the news she wanted to hear. If Mr. Jacobs—Dan—went out a lot, that meant she'd have to stay *in* a lot. Unless, of course, the twins were allowed to go more places by themselves this summer. Sam crossed her fingers and hoped.

"So, I'll see you later," Becky said, heading for the door. She turned back to Sam. "It's been kind of lonely since Allie went to la-la land," Becky said, gesturing to her head meaningfully.

Sam opened one of her suitcases, then decided she'd call Emma and Carrie first. She padded into the hall and dialed the Hewitt residence, where Emma was employed by Jane and Jeff Hewitt. Sam smiled—the phone number had come back into her brain as if she had dialed it yesterday.

9

"Hewitt residence," came Emma's voice.

"Emma! It's me!" Sam called into the phone.

"You're here!" Emma responded happily.

"Wow, I just can't believe it! It's so cool that we're all back!" Sam yelled.

"I know!" Emma agreed. "Carrie and I were just saying the same thing. She just came over."

"Put her on!" Sam demanded.

"Is this the hottest redhead in America who is not already famous?" came Carrie's teasing voice through the phone.

"Hey, the summer is young!" came Sam's laughing retort. "Who knows how notorious I'll be by the end of August?"

"With you," Carrie said, "nothing would surprise me."

"Is Emma as gorgeous as ever?" Sam asked.

"More," Carrie said truthfully.

"Figures," Sam said. "When did you guys get in?"

"I got here yesterday," Carrie said. "Emma's been here for a few days. I don't think she was lonely, though. She's already seen Kurt twice."

Kurt Ackerman was Emma's boyfriend from the previous summer. He was putting himself through college by working as a swimming instructor at the Sunset Country Club and driving a taxi. Although Emma and Kurt really loved each other, the differences in their backgrounds kept getting in the way.

"So are they a hot item or what?" Sam asked, pushing some stray curls behind one ear.

"I don't know. Let me ask her," Carrie said. "Hey, Em, are you and Kurt an item?" Sam heard Carrie ask.

"Maybe," Emma said in the background.

"She said—" Carrie began.

"I heard her," Sam said. "Tell her I expect much better dish than that when I see her. So, when are we getting together? Can we hang out tonight?"

"I think so," Carrie said. "That's what Emma and I were just talking about. How about the Play Café at eight?"

"You got it," Sam answered. "I am so psyched to see you guys!" she added before she hung up.

Sam strolled back into her room and began unpacking her clothes. She knew they wouldn't stay on the hangers for long—she was not known for her neatness—but a clean start seemed like a good idea.

After a hot shower, Sam changed into some cutoffs and a T-shirt from Stingray's, a club she used to go to in Orlando. She found Mr. Jacobs in the den reading a self-improvement book.

"All freshened up, eh?" he asked, putting down the book.

"Yep, I unpacked all my stuff," Sam answered, sitting on the couch. "It feels great to be back."

Mr. Jacobs smiled. "I'm really glad you feel that way, Sam. You know, after the girls started back to school last fall, I began to realize what a positive influence you had been on them."

Sam smiled modestly and tried to look serious. *Positive influence?* What about the time last summer when she had posed for modeling photos in sleazy see-through lingerie, and huge enlargements had been displayed without her knowledge at a local X-rated club? Mr. Jacobs had almost fired her. Well, if he had developed amnesia about that little incident, she was not about to remind him.

"Thanks," Sam said. "They seem much more . . . um . . . grown-up this summer."

"Well, they are fourteen," Mr. Jacobs said

thoughtfully. "And as I said to you on the phone, we need to tread carefully with this whole au pair idea."

"I understand," Sam said, nodding. She was extremely anxious to agree to whatever Mr. Jacobs's plans were for her. At first she hadn't been sure that he would want her back this summer—after all, the girls really *were* much older than the kids her friends were taking care of. On the other hand, once she had gotten fired from Disney World and spent a few months waitressing, working for Mr. Jacobs on Sunset Island had sounded like heaven on earth.

"On the other hand," Mr. Jacobs continued, "the girls aren't nearly as mature as they think they are. And then there's this phase Allie is going through."

"Phase?" Sam echoed politely.

"During the winter she started ranting and raving that she needed her own identity," Mr. Jacobs explained. "She said she was sick of being mistaken for Becky and vice versa. She tried being preppy for about a month and bought an entire wardrobe from L. L. Bean. *Then* she got hooked on reruns of *The Flying Nun*. Now she thinks she has a spiritual calling."

"Give me back my hair dryer, you ugly warthog!" came a shriek from upstairs.

"I see Becky hasn't found the same calling," Sam said with a rueful smile.

"That was Allie," Dan said. "I recognize her voice." He shrugged. "Being spiritual twenty-four hours a day is very hard on her."

Sam choked back a laugh.

"Anyway," Dan continued, "we'll kind of play it by ear. At this point, though, I don't want them staying alone at night. Not unless I'm going to be in by, say, nine o'clock or so."

Sam nodded in agreement. *Oh, just great*, she was thinking. *He's going to be out partying and I'm going to be stuck here with Madonna and the Flying Nun.*

"So, that's about it for now," Dan continued. "Sound cool?"

Sound cool? Mr. Jacobs was asking her if it sounded cool? Even his vocabulary had changed in the past year!

"Sure, sounds . . . uh . . . cool," Sam agreed.

She went upstairs to get ready to meet Carrie and Emma. After pawing through her clothes, she decided on a well-worn pair of jeans, a man's T-shirt, and a black leather motorcycle jacket with a picture of Minnie Mouse painted on the back. The jacket had been a going-away present from her sort-of boyfriend in Orlando—Danny Franklin.

Sam surveyed her reflection in the mirror. Her tall, slender, small-busted frame could carry almost any kind of clothes, but she had developed her own unique style, about which she felt totally confident. Sam fluffed her curls out so they looked even wilder and fastened a rhinestone pin to her motorcycle jacket. *Looking good, girl,* she told her reflection.

Now if only she were half as confident about the rest of her life as she was about her wardrobe, she'd be fine.

TWO

Sam walked into the Play Café precisely at eight o'clock. *Hey, I'm good*, she thought. *Last summer I would have been at least half an hour late!* And on the way over, she had gotten more than her share of male attention. *Nice to know that I haven't been forgotten*, she thought as a coy smile played over her lips.

"Hey, Big Red!" Sam heard a voice call out from behind her. Sam made a face—she hated being called that. She turned around, prepared to take on whatever lame brain guy it was.

It was Carrie, and she was cracking up. Carrie jumped out of her seat and threw her arms around Sam. "That was my best jerky-guy imitation. What did you think?"

"I think you're a moron, but I am *so* glad to see you!" Sam said with a laugh, hugging

17

Carrie back. Sam held her friend out at arm's length. "Whoa, get down, girl! You look great!"

"Thanks," Carrie said, smiling happily. "I lost some weight—healthfully this time," she added meaningfully.

Sam hugged her again. Even Carrie, it turned out, wasn't perfect. When Sam had last seen her over spring break, Carrie had been stressed out from school and was literally making herself sick trying to control her weight. Sam was glad to hear that Carrie had her act together again.

Sam eyed Carrie's outfit, a cotton skirt and T-shirt under an old college varsity jacket. "Listen," Sam began, "I'd kill small children for a jacket like that. Where'd you find it? Can you get me one?"

"Not really," Carrie replied sheepishly. "I found it upstairs in the attic, in a trunk of my dad's stuff."

"Some dad!" Sam exclaimed. "Does he have another? Does he accept bribes?"

Carrie laughed. "Sam, you haven't changed. And speaking of jackets, since when do you own a motorcycle jacket?" She eyed Sam's black leather model.

"Oh, you didn't see the best part of it!" Sam said, twirling around.

"Minnie Mouse! I love it!" Carrie said. "Tell you what—we'll just trade jackets sometime, how's that?"

"Deal," Sam said, sliding into the booth. "Have you seen the blond Boston baroness?"

"There she is." Carrie pointed to the door.

"Emma bo-bemma!" Sam shouted happily. "Come and join the other two musketeers."

Emma's face broke into a smile. The summer before, Emma had really come into her own, Sam thought. When they had first met, Emma had been afraid that people would think of her as a spoiled rich girl whose parents hobnobbed with the Kennedys. On the other hand, by virtue of her patrician upbringing, she could tell an obnoxious guy to take a long walk off a short pier in five different languages—a skill that had stood her in good stead!

"Sam, I am soooo glad we're all here," Emma said. "And guess what—Jeff and Jane are going to give me an extra night off every week this summer, as a special reward for deciding to come back."

Sam groaned. "After I switch jackets with Carrie, let me switch families with you. You guys aren't going to believe what's going on in the nutso Jacobs household." Sam proceeded to tell Emma and Carrie the story of how the Jacobs family had been utterly transformed.

"So it's like this," Sam said. "Mr. Jacobs has practically rebuilt his body. He could be a contestant on *American Gladiators*. Allie now looks like an unhappy flower child but talks like my old Sunday school teacher, and Becky looks like she's vying for the title of Girl Most Likely to Commit a Major Felony. The question is, what am *I* going to look like at the end of this summer . . . if I survive these people, that is?"

Emma and Carrie cracked up.

Patsi, the waitress who had worked at the Play Café the previous summer, came over to the girls' table. "Nice to see you guys yukking it up," she said, "but are you about ready to order? There's always a big rush when the movies let out." She pulled out her pencil. "Good to see you guys again," she added.

"Uh, excuse me, Patsi," Sam said mischievously, "but wasn't last summer supposed to be your last summer working here? I mean, I know it's hard to tear yourself away from the delights of waitressing at the Play Café, but I thought you were going to go to Europe with your earnings, girlfriend."

Patsi sighed. "'Europe' is parked in the lot out back. Sue me. I have a weakness for red sports cars," she said, smiling. "Anyway, the plates on it say *Europe*, and may I please take your order?"

Sam ordered her usual double cheeseburger, fries, and a Coke. Emma got a small Greek salad and a ginger ale, while Carrie ordered a shrimp salad sandwich and an iced tea.

"So, Emma," Sam said with a conspiratorial wink, "nice to see that you're drinking ginger ale." Emma had been upset about her family during their last reunion and had starting drinking excessive amounts of wine. Sam knew that Emma's parents were not the easiest people to deal with—Sam had met Emma's mother—but was glad to see that Emma, too, was herself again. *After all*, Sam thought, *I'm supposed to be the one who doesn't know what's happening next!*

"I am, as they say, clean and sober," Emma said. "Anyway, I've decided I should put my energies into something more constructive—namely shopping."

Sam groaned. "On a limitless budget! There is no justice in this world."

"Oh, come on," Emma said. "You manage

to look incredibly sexy and totally unique no matter what. And I still don't know how you do it!" she added with a laugh.

"Fashion guts," Sam said definitively. "Supposedly it makes up for bucks. Anyhow, you look unbelievable and perfect, per usual. If anything, you're in better shape than when I saw you a few months ago. Look at those triceps!"

Emma was wearing a sleeveless cobalt-blue cotton minidress with matching flats. As usual, she was slightly overdressed for the island, and, as usual, there was no one in the Play Café who could come close to her in class.

"Well, I started working out in the weight room at Goucher," Emma said. "I was hoping that the results would be starting to show."

"Stick with me," Sam said, "eat everything that I eat, and I guarantee that whatever progress you made will just melt away."

Carrie poked Sam in the ribs. Sam was famous for being able to consume mountains of food without it showing at all. Carrie had to watch what she ate all the time, and Emma just naturally had a small appetite.

"Hey, Big Red!" For the second time that

evening Sam heard a voice call out to her. And this time it wasn't Carrie or Emma doing the calling. This time there were two seriously cute guys walking toward them—Pres (short for Presley) Travis and Billy Sampson.

Pres and Billy were part of one of the hottest new rock bands in New England, Flirting with Danger, known to their fans as just the Flirts. The summer before, Carrie and sandy-haired lead singer Billy had become a hot couple—he'd even invited her to come to Bangor for one of his gigs. Carrie liked Billy a lot, but was still trying to figure out what to do about Josh, her old boyfriend from New Jersey. Sometimes she was afraid that what she felt for Billy was just lust, and that her feeling for Josh was something more real. On the other hand, whenever she was in Billy's presence she felt like she would melt on the spot. And that was hard to resist just because she was supposed to be level-headed and mature.

As for Pres, a tall, sexy, long-haired guy from Tennessee, Sam was quite taken with him, but their relationship had consisted mainly of flirting. Pres made Sam laugh, satisfying her most important requirement in men—after how they filled out a pair of tight jeans, of course.

"Hey, ladies," Pres greeted them in his typical Southern fashion. "Y'all look real fine settin' there."

Sam didn't miss the fact that Pres's eyes were clearly focused on her and her alone.

Out of the corner of her eye she also watched Billy, who had just sneaked up behind Carrie and kissed her on the neck. Sam hooted, and Carrie blushed.

Billy laughed. "You weren't supposed to see that, Sam." He winked at her and Emma.

Emma answered by clinking her glass with a spoon loudly enough to get the attention of everyone in their corner of the Play Café. Sam and Carrie watched their friend in amazement as she stood up. *What happened to conservative, reserved Emma?* Sam wondered.

"Ladies and gentlemen," Emma announced, "it gives me great pleasure to introduce Ms. Samantha Bridges, who will propose the evening's toast."

Sam's jaw dropped open, but she had no choice but to stand up. Emma clearly had had some practice at this sort of thing.

Well, I'm not known for being timid myself, Sam thought. "Ladies and gentlemen, and Emma Cresswell," she started—

everyone cracked up—"I would like to propose a toast to several of my favorite things in life. To my best friends, Carrie and Emma, for demonstrating great wisdom and obedience to me by returning to Sunset Island."

Emma and Carrie booed and hissed good-naturedly.

"To the good-looking men of the world, present company included, for having had the good sense to be on this planet at the same time as me," Sam continued.

Pres and Billy took a bow.

"And to the Hewitts, the Jacobses, and the Templetons, for offering us substantial increase in salary and substantial lessening of our duties as au pairs this summer . . . in our dreams," Sam concluded with a flourish.

"Hear, hear!" Emma cried.

"I'd like to propose somethin'," Pres said. "I propose that Billy and I mosey over to that empty pool table so that I can do to him what Carrie did to Butchie last summer." Pres was referring to how Carrie had out-hustled the biggest pool hustler on the island and taken him for a hundred dollars . . . and his dignity. It had been the talk of the island for the rest of the summer.

25

"Proposal accepted," Billy replied. "I hope you brought your lucky pool cue with you because you're gonna need all the help you can get. Excuse me, ladies. You too, Sam," Billy added with a wink, and Billy and Pres walked over to the table.

"What a couple of hunks!" Sam cried when they were barely out of earshot. "I don't know which of them looks better, Pres or Billy. What do you think, Emma?"

"I think . . . I think . . . well, neither of them is Kurt, you know." Emma blushed.

"Whoa, Emma, tell it like it be!" Sam guffawed. "All I know is that I wouldn't be bored if all I had to do this summer is follow those two around."

"Hey, you are not one to follow *anyone* around," Carrie reminded Sam with a laugh.

"True," Sam agreed. "On second thought, they should follow *me* around . . . backwards!"

"What I mean, oh ye of the one-track mind," Carrie continued, "is that you might actually have to do a little work while you're here."

"Thank you, Little Miss Responsibility," Sam said with a groan.

"Carrie's right," Emma said. "And then there's making plans for the fall—you have to do that, too," she added.

26

Sam rolled her eyes. "It's the first day of summer, you guys. Can't this wait until the end of August?"

"It's a little difficult to make plans on August thirtieth for what you're going to do on August thirty-first," Emma said.

"Hey, you guys, I'm an impetuous woman. Leave me alone!" Sam cried. "It's easy for you to talk—college just skips right along, year after year. You don't even have to make any decisions!"

"That's not exactly true," Emma said. "I did survive one year at Goucher, so I suppose I could survive another. But what I'm thinking about doing is taking part in this exchange program they have, where sophomores can go abroad for a year of independent study."

"What's the big deal?" Sam asked. "You've already been all over the world—first class, I might add."

"This would be different," Emma said, her eyes shining. "You know how I keep talking about the Peace Corps·and Africa . . ."

"And how you never have the nerve to do anything about it," Sam added, quoting what Emma herself had often admonished herself for.

"Shhh!" Carrie hissed, poking her in the ribs again.

"Well, I can arrange to go to Africa next year as part of this program!"

"Hey, that's great!" said Carrie.

"It really is," Sam said. "It's what you've always said you wanted."

"Of course, I'll still have to deal with my parents' reaction," Emma said, "but that really *is* something that can wait until the end of the summer!"

"Food, glorious food!" Patsi sang out as she delivered their orders to them. "Chow down!"

Sam turned to Carrie and blew her straw wrapper at her friend's face. "I suppose you have every moment of your perfect life planned out for the fall, too, huh?"

"My life, as you know, is far from perfect," Carrie reminded her, throwing the wrapper back at Sam playfully. "I'll go back to Yale, of course. Meanwhile, I plan to make this summer as much of an escape from the real world as I can."

"I'll drink to that!" Sam cried, lifting her glass of Coke. "I'm all for escaping from the real world!"

"Yes, but *you* try to make it permanent," Emma said, unfolding her napkin and draping it on her lap.

Carrie took a bite of her sandwich and

looked at Sam. "I don't suppose you have plans for anything as mundane as going back to college, do you?"

Sam leaned forward and motioned her friends to put their heads close to hers, as if she had something so important to say that no one else in the Play Café could possibly be permitted to hear it.

"Ladies, this year, following a wild, uninhibited, and altogether legendary summer on Sunset Island, I, Samantha Bridges, intend to . . . become a drill sergeant in the United States Marine Corps." Sam burst out laughing, and Emma and Carrie joined in.

"No, really, Sam," Carrie said. "Have you thought at all about what you're going to do in September?"

"Like I said, I'm going to join the circus and be one of the ladies who ride the elephants. I've already talked it over with Danny, and he said that he would walk behind the elephants to sweep up if I was the one doing the riding!"

"Sam!" Carrie said, exasperated.

"Hey, cut me some slack, okay?" Sam joked. "I'm a confused post-adolescent who's been stupefied by Presley Travis's buns!"

"Okay," Emma said. "But I'm not going to let you avoid this subject the whole summer.

It's too important. Anyway, how is Danny?"

Sam told her friends the latest about Danny, whom she had met while they were both working at Disney World the past fall. Sam had been a dancer in one of the stage shows, but had gotten fired because her dancing, though good, was too original. Danny, who spent the working day dressed as the cartoon character Goofy, was her best friend and confidante in the world beside Carrie and Emma. Sam remembered that she had never thought she could be romantically involved with a friend . . . until she had kissed Danny.

"So, I like him. Correction, I really, *really* like him," Sam confessed. "But I don't know. He's there, I'm here . . ."

"Sometimes I think you don't really want a boyfriend," Emma said thoughtfully.

"Ah well, you know me," Sam said. "So many men, so little time—that's my motto."

"Maybe," Emma said, "but maybe you're just afraid of getting hurt."

"Whoa, heavy conversation alert!" Sam sang out a bit too loudly. Emma was hitting a little too close to home, and Sam was not in the mood for true confessions.

"Hey, look," Carrie said, pointing in the direction of the pool table, where Pres and

Billy had just won a game from two tourists. "They're waving at us to come over and dance with them. Want to?"

"Let's!" Sam said.

All three walked over to the Play Café's small dance floor. A hot Tanya Tucker tune was playing on the eclectic jukebox, and couples were getting up from all over the café to go boogie. Sam, Emma, Carrie, Billy, and Pres commandeered one corner of the floor and got down. Sam, especially, really cut loose.

"Wow, Sam, you were always hands down the best dancer of all of us, but now you've gotten amazing!" Emma yelled over the music to her friend.

"It's all those months of pirouetting to 'It's a Small World After All,'" Sam shouted back, then executed a particularly stunning double turn. "It took me to a whole new creative level!"

By now, people all over the Play Café were pointing and staring. Sam Bridges, who had made a name for herself on the island the summer before with her red cowboy boots and outrageous getups, was in the process of making a name for herself for her dancing pizzaz and ability. She was fabulous.

"Hey, Big Red!" Sam heard for the third

time that evening. But this time it was a couple of women's voices chiming in unison. Sam groaned. She recognized the voices. Then she tapped Emma and Carrie on the shoulder, and they turned to meet the chorus together.

It was Lorell Courtland and Diana De Witt, their archenemies from the previous summer. Diana knew Emma from boarding school, and had blown Emma's cover when Emma was trying to keep her family's wealth a secret. Diana had come to the island as Lorell's houseguest, and had liked it so much that she had stayed for the entire summer. They were rich, obnoxious, perfectly groomed, and totally hateful, and went out of their way to make life miserable for them.

In fact, that past winter, when Sam, Emma, and Carrie had been together at a big Graham Perry concert in Miami, Lorell had turned up at a private party on Graham's yacht with the despicable Flash Hathaway, the sleazy photographer who had taken the nearly nude photos of Sam. And when the three friends had been "accidentally" set adrift in a small dinghy attached to the yacht, they strongly suspected that Lorell had had something to do with it.

"Say it ain't so!" Sam groaned to Carrie and Emma. "It's the two-headed she-monster from hell. Aaaghhh!" she screamed in mock fright.

Lorell and Diana slowly made their way over to the girls on the dance floor.

"It's my favorite threesome!" Lorell drawled sarcastically in her syrupy Southern voice. She looked Emma, Carrie, and Sam up and down disdainfully as they danced. Diana stood just behind her, smiling a nasty smile. "Still dressing as tackily as ever, I see," she continued, directing her gaze at Sam.

"I have an idea," Emma said, her face composed and friendly. "Since you two are so rich, why don't you just tell your daddies to buy you some other nice little island? That way you won't ruin our view all summer long."

"Why, Emma Cresswell, what an unladylike thing to say, especially when we know your daddy could do the same," Diana chided. "And we all know what a lady you are. You probably drive your car with your ankles crossed."

The song ended and the girls stood still on the dance floor.

"Look, this is ridiculous," Carrie said,

pushing her hair off her face. "Let's not spend another summer feuding. It's such a waste of time, don't you think?"

"*Au contraire*," Lorell purred with a nasty smile. "The three of you add such *comedy* to our lives. We'd be simply lost without y'all."

Diana nodded in agreement. "It's sort of a Three Stooges, *Hee Haw* kind of thing," she mused. "I personally find you three irresistible."

"Well, could y'all find them irresistible at a distance? We're tryin' to dance here," Pres said in his soft drawl.

Diana looked Pres over meaningfully. She licked her lips. "Sure thing, cowboy. I'll be seeing you later. Bye, darlings!"

Diana and Lorell turned and sauntered off.

Carrie was shaking her head in disgust, Emma was fuming, and Sam was trying to shrug them off. But as she started dancing again she couldn't help notice that Pres's eyes were following Diana across the room.

THREE

The next day dawned bright and sunny. Sam had already made arrangements with Mr. Jacobs to take the twins to the Sunset Country Club for the day, even though Becky had protested that she and her sister were perfectly capable of going to the club on their own. Mr. Jacobs, however, insisted that Sam drive them there. *That's fine with me*, thought Sam. *It will give me a chance to meet whatever college guys have transformed themselves from nerds to hunks during the school year.*

Becky was out of the car even before they came to a full stop in the club parking lot. "See you later, Sam," she yelled. "I'm going to see how my new bathing suit gets reviewed!" Becky had on a white crocheted bikini with a thong bottom, which Sam suspected would get good reviews indeed. "Allie, hurry up!" Becky shouted.

"I'm going to find a meditation tree," Allie said. "I haven't spent any time today contemplating the nature of the universe."

Becky shrugged and grabbed her towel and beachbag. "If I had on the bathing suit you're wearing, I'd hide out behind a tree, too." Allie was wearing a one-piece bathing suit with a skirt. It covered about ten times the amount of skin as her sister's did, and looked like it belonged on her grandmother, not her.

Once they had passed through the clubhouse, Becky darted straight for the pool, while Allie drifted off toward the small garden near the golf course.

Sam marveled, as she always did, at how amazing a facility this club was. It had golf, swimming, tennis, stables, a complete gym—there was nothing like the Sunset Country Club in Junction, Kansas!

Sam found Emma by the kiddie pool, where she was watching the youngest Hewitt, four-year-old Katie, splash around in the pool. The two older kids, Wills and Ethan, were swimming laps in the main pool.

"Hey, Emma, nice suit you got on, chiquita! Very south-of-France!" Sam said as she strode over to her friend. Emma was wearing a ribbed yellow tank suit that showed off her aerobicized figure perfectly.

"Thanks, Sam." Emma smiled. "Why don't you come sit with us? Kurt just went inside to get a couple of sodas."

Sam plopped down on the end of Emma's chaise longue. "Don't mind if I do," she said. "So how are you two getting along?" she asked, pulling out her suntan lotion.

"Well, I'm awfully happy to be with him again," Emma said with a blissful little smile on her face.

"Yes, but would you be awfully happy to go all the way with him?" Sam asked. "Because as I told you, I will never forgive you if you lose your virginity before I do."

"Sam Bridges, if you open a dictionary and look up the word *impossible*, you'll find your photo as the definition!" Emma said with a giggle. "Anyway," she said, spreading more sunblock on her upper arms, "I've made a decision. I've decided that it's going to be a long summer, that I've just arrived, and that there's no good reason to hurry. I mean, this is an island, and Kurt and I are both here, aren't we?"

"Meaning you and I get to remain the two

most virtuous women on this island—for the time being, anyway."

"When it's the right time with Kurt, I'll know it," Emma affirmed.

"Speaking of the devil, here he comes—looking as fine as ever, I might add. Hey, Kurt!"

"Hey, Sam! Welcome back to the island!" Kurt said, giving Sam a friendly hug. "Emma told me you were going to be back on Sunset Island this summer, and I can tell you just how happy she is that you're here." Kurt put the drinks down on a small table.

"Right," Emma agreed, but she couldn't tear her gaze away from Kurt's face. Her smile could have outshone the sun. Kurt gazed back at her with equal happiness. Suddenly Sam felt like the proverbial fifth wheel.

"Well, I'll just leave you two lovebirds alone," Sam said, standing up and stretching. "Time for me to make sure the Flying Nun, Allie Jacobs, hasn't gone wandering off in search of the Holy Grail."

"I haven't even seen her yet this summer," Kurt said.

"You wouldn't recognize her if you had," Sam said. "Emma will fill you in on the gruesome details."

Sam walked away toward the garden and found Allie under a stately oak tree, writing furiously in a notebook.

"Hey, Allie, what are you writing?" Sam asked as she approached.

"Samantha, please don't interrupt. I'm thinking great thoughts," Allie replied, not lifting her head.

"Okay." Sam shrugged. "When you're ready to trade in your pen for a chicken salad sandwich for lunch, I'll treat!"

When Sam arrived back at poolside, Becky spotted her and waved from over near the lifeguard stand. "Sam!" Becky yelled to her. "Come here, there's someone incredibly cool I want you to meet."

As Sam walked over to Becky, the younger girl pointed up. In the lifeguard chair was a girl about Sam's age whom she had never seen before. The lifeguard had incredibly thick and long dark hair tied back in a ponytail.

"Sam, this is Marina Mazzetti," Becky called up proudly. "She's a dancer from New York City. Marina, this is Samantha Bridges—Sam. She's our—um, a friend of mine."

Marina looked quickly at the pool, saw that it was temporarily empty, and then climbed gracefully down from the chair. She took off her sunglasses and stuck a hand out to Sam. "Pleased to meet you. Becky here is a big fan of yours."

"Really?" Sam said in a wry voice, shooting Becky a look of surprise.

"Don't look so shocked," Becky said. "You have your moments."

Sam shook her head and noticed Marina's nails glinting in the sun. "Wow, awesome manicure," Sam said, fixing her gaze on Marina's hands. Marina had the longest, most perfectly manicured nails Sam had ever seen. And on each pinky nail were eight rhinestones laid out in the shape of a star. "Did you get your manicure on the island?"

"Are you kidding?" Marina replied, her eyes going back and forth from Sam to the pool. "No, there's a Korean manicure shop around the corner from the studio where I rehearse. The owner does my nails for half price because every now and then I bring her a panful of my special lasagna. How I'm gonna do the upkeep on them here on this island, I'll never know," she added with a sigh. "Hey, no running by the pool!" Marina screamed at two kids who skidded by. "Listen, I gotta get back to work. Do you want to talk later? I get a lunch break in twenty minutes."

"Sure," Sam agreed. "The pizza here is pretty good."

"Yeah? So we'll split one," Marina suggested.

"Well, actually, shocking as it may seem, I can eat a whole one by myself," Sam admitted.

Marina laughed. "Trust me, I don't shock easily. I'm from Brooklyn."

Sam had already gotten a table in the big country club restaurant when Marina came in. Marina had pulled on a pair of Levi's and a Vertical Club staff T-shirt. Sam noticed how cute Marina was as she walked toward her. She was about five feet five inches tall, with that gorgeous long, thick, black hair, and a slender but very curvy figure. Sam sighed at the way Marina filled out her T-shirt, and then looked down at her own small chest. *Hey, who cares?* Sam told herself with a mental shrug. *I've got other ace qualities.*

As Marina stopped to pick up a paper cup someone had dropped, Sam couldn't help but notice how graceful she was. *This girl can move,* Sam thought. *Becky said she's a dancer. I wouldn't be surprised if she's really good.*

Sam waved to her. Marina saw her immediately, came over, and sat down. "So, big eater, where are the two pizzas?" Marina asked with a grin.

"I was waiting for you," Sam replied, "and checking out the local male talent. I must say that if you're looking to meet guys on this island, this club is either sink or swim. And today it's sink."

Marina cracked up. She reached for a menu and said, "Sam, where I live in New York, you get so much male attention on the street that it makes you want to put a muzzle on every male member of the species."

"My kind of town!" Sam joked.

"Not really," Marina said. "You can't imagine how old it gets. So, are we going for the pizza or what?"

"With everything?" Sam asked with a wide grin.

"My kind of woman," Marina agreed.

Sam got the waitress's attention and ordered two pies.

"It'll be a little while," Sam cautioned Marina. "They're not exactly famous for fast service here."

"Just like the restaurant at the Vertical Club in Manhattan," Marina said. "They think they're doing you a favor to let you order lunch."

"What's this Vertical Club?" Sam asked.

"Lemme give you the short version of how I came to be on this island," Marina replied, "because I think someone should do a TV movie about my life. The Vertical Club is this ritzy health club on the Upper East Side of Manhattan where I used to work six days a week teaching the six A.M. and nine A.M. aerobics classes. Lots of fun, considering that I got the great joy of riding the subway from Brooklyn every morning at five. Now, *that* is my idea of a good time."

"Why didn't you just move to Manhattan?" Sam questioned. She took a sip of the ice water the waitress had put on the table. "You'd have gotten a lot more sleep."

"Don't I know it," Marina said. "But who could afford the rents there? I have a friend who lives in a fifth-floor walk-up on East seventh Street, and she's paying around nine-fifty a month in rent."

"Really?" Sam asked, wide-eyed.

Marina nodded. "And listen," she continued, "that doesn't even include utilities. There's no doorman and the buzzer downstairs doesn't work, so she has to throw her keys out her window to anyone who comes to visit."

"So how does she afford that?"

"Dancers usually live about four to a two-bedroom apartment in order to be on the magic island," Marina said with disgust. "She sublets. Even living in Brooklyn I'm totally broke. What with dance classes, stretch classes, voice classes, audition seminars, travel, and clothes, I'm running a deficit."

Sam stared at Marina with fascination. *So this is what it's like to really be an artist in Manhattan*, she thought. "How'd you end up here for the summer?" she asked. "You were going to tell me."

"Oh, that! Sorry, I got on a roll about New York there for a minute. This lady, Mrs. Bauersachs, took my early aerobics class. She and I got to be friends. One day she came to one of my dance recitals and decided I was going to be the next Gelsey Kirkland, though I keep telling her I'm not much interested in ballet. Then she offered to pay for my dance training. And since she's got this estate on the south side of Sunset Island, she and her husband invited me up for the summer. I think I'm supposed to be the kid she never had," Marina concluded.

Sam's jaw had just about hit the table during Marina's story. Marina had a patron! Someone who believed in her as an artist!

"I am incredibly jealous," Sam sighed. "I *dream* of some rich person doing something like that for me! But I thought maybe it only happened in the movies."

"That's what I used to think, too," Marina agreed.

"Pizza delivery," the waitress said as she laid two steaming pies on their table.

"Thanks, Susan," Sam said as the waitress hurried off. "So what do your parents think about your being on the artistic dole?" she asked as she took a piece of the pizza.

"They don't," Marina replied. She bit into a slice.

"What do you mean?" Sam asked. "They've got to think something! They're parents! It's their job in life to harass you!"

"They don't," Marina repeated. "For a good reason. I don't know them."

Sam stared at her new friend. She had no idea what Marina was talking about. *How could anyone not know her parents?* she thought.

"Don't look like I just told you I shot the Pope," Marina joked.

"Well, I mean, I . . ." Sam stammered.

"Hey, it's okay," Marina said. "I'm used to the idea. I don't know who my parents are because I was adopted when I was a baby. Then some social service agency found my adoptive parents to be unfit and took me away. So I lived in a bunch of foster homes until I turned eighteen. That was last year." Marina took another bite of her pizza and made a face. "I gotta tell you, Little Italy this ain't."

"I never would have known," Sam marveled. "That you grew up without real parents, I mean. It's just that . . . well, you seem so together. A dancer in New York, an aerobics teacher, out on your own . . ."

"Everyone loses their parents sometime," Marina said as she ate. "I just lost mine a whole lot earlier than most."

"Yeah, but it must have been so hard," Sam mused.

Marina shrugged. "Just because you have foster parents when you're a kid doesn't mean that you're going to grow up to be a drug addict or a hooker. That seems to be what most people think."

"I wasn't thinking that at all—" Sam began.

"Listen," Marina interrupted, "just be happy you know who your parents are and that they'll be your parents for a long time."

"I am," Sam said emphatically, crumbling the leftover crust from her last slice of pizza. "Well, I try to be, anyway. My parents don't really understand me. They think I should be in college, something I have zero desire to do."

"Neither do I!" Marina exclaimed with a laugh. "So we have something in common."

"Dancing, that's what we really have in common," Sam said. "You must be great if you dance in New York."

"I am great," Marina said, smiling, "or at least that's what I tell myself when I wake up at four in the morning to stretch for an audition and then get there to find some slimy producer who's only interested in the girls who are at least six feet tall and are willing to make nice for a chance to work."

"That's how it is, huh?" Sam asked.

"Sometimes, yes, sometimes no," Marina said. She put down what was left of her last slice of pizza and looked at her watch. "Hey, I gotta get back to work. It was great talking with you."

"Listen, I have an idea," Sam said. "My two best friends and I are going dancing tonight at Bailey's—that new club out by the dock. It's supposed to be really hot. Why don't you come with us?"

"I'd love to," Marina said, throwing down enough money to cover her pizza. "What time?"

"I know where the Bauersachses' estate is," Sam said. "We can pick you up about nine, okay?"

"Cool," Marina agreed. "Oh yeah, one other thing. What's the dress code?"

"Sunset Island chic," Sam replied, "which means you can wear anything you want as long as you think it will make guys fall at your feet."

Marina laughed. "I've got a few outfits that fit the bill. See you later!"

As Sam got ready to go dancing that night, she thought more about Marina. She couldn't imagine what it would be like to grow up without parents or a family. As crazy as her family made her, at least she had one.

Sam surveyed her outfit in the mirror before heading out the door. The pleated white miniskirt above the red cowboy boots showed off her endless legs to great advantage. And the man's suit vest she'd found in an antique-clothing store for two dollars looked very sexy over her naked skin. She spritzed herself with some perfume and shook her curls one last time.

Sam picked up Carrie and Emma and told them about Marina. "You're really going to like her," Sam promised as she headed for the estate where Marina was staying. "She's a professional dancer in New York!"

Marina was ready and waiting when Sam pulled the car up the long drive.

"Hi, guys," Marina said, climbing into the back seat.

Sam introduced everyone.

"Great outfit!" Carrie said, admiring Marina's sleek pink silk slip dress. "I wish I could dress like that."

"Hey, you look great," Emma told Carrie with a smile.

"That's because you lent me your sweater!" Carrie laughed, looking down at the white crocheted sweater with the delicate lace trim. "Is it too tight on me?"

"Very Marilyn Monroe," Sam assured her. "Hey, I actually see a parking spot!" she cried triumphantly as she pulled into the only spot in sight.

As soon as the four girls walked in the front door, the pulsating music overwhelmed them. Where the Play Café had a homey, collegiate sort of atmosphere, Bailey's seemed like a rock-and-roll rocket about to take off.

"I think I drank too much iced tea before," Carrie said. "I've got to run to the ladies' room."

"I'll come with you," Emma said. She turned to Sam and Marina. "We'll be right back. Try not to get into any trouble," she added with a laugh as she walked away.

"Dance?" a guy asked Marina before Emma and Carrie had been gone more than thirty seconds. Sam raised her eyebrows. *She* was used to being the first one guys noticed.

Marina turned to Sam. "Hey, how about you and I dance this one and warm ourselves up for whatever the night has in store, huh?" she asked in a low voice.

"You're on," Sam said, thinking how good she and Marina would look out on the dance floor, boogieing together.

"Sorry," Marina called to the guy. "Maybe later."

Sam and Marina hit the dance floor, and it was destined never to be the same again. Both spectacular dancers, but with completely different styles and looks, they quickly took over while the rest of the crowd moved back to watch them. It turned into a friendly sort of competition, each egging the other on to even more awesome dance moves. When the song finished, there were whoops and whistles from the crowd. Flushed from the exertion, Sam looked around and saw Carrie and Emma standing on the balcony, giving her a thumbs-up sign.

"Excuse me, ladies, I'm Jack Germaine," a nicely dressed older man said, tapping Marina on the shoulder. "Call me Jack."

"Yeah?" Marina said over the music, which had started up again.

"You two are fabulous dancers!" he yelled.

"Thanks!" Sam said. She never got tired of hearing it.

"I really mean it," Jack continued. "You're both terrific. Outstanding!"

Sam smiled some more, but she thought the guy was laying it on a little thick. Still, he was older than anyone else in the club. Maybe he just thought he had to try harder.

"Well, excuse us!" Marina yelled so Jack could hear her. She grabbed Sam's arm and started to move away.

"Just one thing," Jack said, stopping them. "How would you both like jobs as professional dancers?"

FOUR

"Say *what?*" Marina said, her hands on her hips.

"I said—listen, it's too noisy to talk here. Let's go over by the bar."

Sam looked at Marina, Marina looked at Sam, and they both shrugged.

Oh well, Sam thought, *I have nothing to lose.* She motioned to Emma and Carrie that she'd be right back, and then she followed Marina and Jack Germaine across the floor to the bar.

"There, that's better," Jack said. "At least I can hear myself think." He smiled at Sam and Marina. "So, what can I get you two ladies to drink?"

"Nothing," Marina answered, speaking for both of them. "What kind of a scam are you running, exactly?"

Jack just laughed. He didn't seem to take

offense. Sam was glad. On that one chance in a million that this was something legit, she didn't want Marina to blow it.

"Listen, I don't blame you for being skeptical. Let me explain," Jack said. "I work for Show World International. We're promoters out of New York with a regional office in Bangor," he explained.

"Yeah, well, I live in New York and I've never heard of you," Marina said disdainfully.

This time Sam kicked Marina ever so subtly. *No use in offending the guy right off the bat*, she figured.

"Have you heard of every promoter in New York?" Jack asked, arching his eyebrows.

"No, I guess not," Marina admitted.

"We hire dancers for clubs, some in the U.S., a lot of them in Japan and the Middle East."

"No kidding?" Sam said, instantly intrigued.

"No kidding," Jack said. "We've given a lot of girls their big break."

The words *big break* echoed in Sam's head. *That's what I'm waiting for! That's what I really need!* she thought excitedly. On the other hand, she wasn't some stupid, innocent kid anymore, ready to believe some guy's line at a bar. She was, however, ready to listen to what Jack had to say.

"Many of our girls have gone on to dance in Vegas and in Broadway shows," Jack continued.

"Wow, that's great!" Sam said.

This time it was Marina's turn to kick Sam. "So what does this have to do with us?" Marina asked.

"Well, nothing, unless either of you is interested in dancing professionally."

"We might be," Marina said evenly.

"We're holding regional auditions for some of our overseas shows this Saturday at two o'clock at the Dance Loft in Bangor," Jack said. "Here, I'll write down the information for you." Jack took out a business card with an embossed logo on the front. He scribbled some information on the back and handed the card to Sam.

Marina was still skeptical. "Do you, like, hang out in clubs giving this line to girls, or what?"

Jack smiled. "I have been known to find talent in clubs," he agreed easily. "But, hey, where else would you find dancers except at a place to dance?"

"That's true," Sam said eagerly.

"So, I hope to see you girls there," Jack said, cordially shaking their hands. He turned and started away from them, but Marina's voice stopped him.

"Hey, Jack, just one last teeny thing," she called to him. "These dancers you hire would be dancing with their clothes *on*, wouldn't they?"

"You betcha," Jack assured her. "We hire dancers, not strippers."

Sam looked down at the card in her hand. "Hey, this is way cool, don't you think?"

"What I *think* is that it's some kind of scam," Marina said, checking the polish on her fingernails.

"Who was that guy?" Carrie asked as she bopped over to them. She lifted her hair and fanned the back of her neck.

"Just the question I was about to ask," said Emma, coming up behind her.

Sam thrust the business card at Carrie. "He says he hires dancers for shows overseas," Sam said. "There's an audition Saturday in Bangor."

"Why is the name Flash Hathaway jumping into my mind?" Emma said, looking coolly over Carrie's shoulder at the business card.

"Oh, come on, I was a *child* then," Sam scoffed.

"Yeah, well, *this* child is gonna check the dude out," Marina said. "I'll make a few phone calls to some friends in New York, get the lowdown on the lowlife . . ."

"What if he isn't a lowlife?" Sam said. "It *is* possible, you know. We really are good dancers."

Marina grinned an infectious grin. "Too true."

"You guys aren't really thinking of going to this audition, are you?" Carrie asked them.

"Maybe," Sam said. "Why not?"

"Because he's just some guy in a club!" Carrie exclaimed.

"And I'm just some girl in a club, is that it?" Sam asked. "Don't you think it's possible he thinks that we're exceptional dancers?"

"Of course you're an exceptional dancer," Emma said. "You, too, Marina, but—"

"Time out, you two," Marina interrupted. "No offense, but I'm not exactly used to my friends making my decisions for me. So I'll check the guy out, and we'll see. Cool?"

"Okay," Carrie echoed reluctantly.

Emma nodded in agreement.

"I really can take care of myself, you guys," Sam told them.

"Excuse me," came a sexy, low male voice

from behind Sam. She turned around. A guy about her height with white-blond hair and a deep, dark tan stood there smiling at her. "I saw you dancing before. You're awesome."

Sam flipped a significant look at her friends. "Thanks," she said smugly.

"My name's Taylor. Want to dance?"

"Sure," Sam said easily. "Excuse me," she told Emma and Carrie. "Duty calls."

Taylor turned out to be a terrific dancer himself. Between dances, he told Sam that he was a sophomore at the University of Maine and that he was vacationing on the island with his parents for two weeks. He told her his girlfriend of three years, Wendy, had just broken up with him, and he would do anything to get her back. He said his heart was mending slowly. When a slow tune came on, though, he had obviously mended enough to take Sam close into his arms.

"Mmm, this feels nice," Taylor breathed into Sam's hair. "*You* feel nice."

Sam rolled her eyes. *Guys.* They were impossible. One minute they wanted to cry on your shoulder over their lost love, and the next minute she was completely forgotten because they wanted to get into your pants.

"Want to go for a walk on the beach?" Taylor asked Sam hopefully when the song finished.

"No thanks," Sam said. "I'm going to call it a night."

"So, can I call you?" Taylor asked.

"I don't think so," Sam said. "Hey, nice meeting you. Good luck with Wendy," she added pointedly.

Sam found Emma, Carrie, and Marina just coming out of the ladies' room.

"I'm ready to book," Sam said. "Much as I hate to contemplate it, I'm supposed to get up for breakfast with the monsters at eight o'clock. Of course Allie gets up at six so she can do her morning prayers," she added, shaking her head.

"I'm ready, too," Emma said.

Carrie and Marina decided to leave as well, and they all headed out to the parking lot.

"So you'll do some checking tomorrow about this Show World International thing?" Sam asked, turning around to look at Marina.

"Absolutely," Marina confirmed.

"Just be careful, you two," Carrie said.

"Yes, Mom," Sam answered playfully. She crossed her fingers and looked out at the starry night. Maybe this guy *was* legit. Stranger things had happened. Maybe this really *would* be her big break.

"Sam, do you believe in God?"

"Huh? Wha?" Sam asked sleepily. She came fuzzily awake. Allie was sitting at the foot of Sam's bed, dressed in a flannel nightgown that buttoned up to her chin.

"Do you believe in God?" Allie asked again.

Sam sat up and rubbed the sleep out of her eyes. "Isn't it a little early for this?"

"If we don't think about our immortal souls now, it may be too late," Allie said pointedly.

Sam sighed and tried to ignore the cottony feeling in her mouth. *This is no way to wake up*, she thought. "Well, actually, Allie, I'm not sure what I believe. That's the truth."

"Me neither," Allie admitted. "Please don't tell anyone," she added seriously.

"Hey, Allie, it's okay. At least you're actually thinking about these things, which is more than most people can say."

"Don't tell anyone that I've got any doubts. Promise?" Allie asked, anxiety etched across her face.

Sam patted Allie's flannel-clad knee. "I won't tell anyone," she assured her. "Have you thought about talking to your rabbi?"

"I did," Allie said with disgust. "He said it's okay to have doubts, too. He told me I was going through a phase. Don't you just hate it when adults tell you you're going through a phase?"

"Yeah, it's the worst," Sam agreed.

Allie got up and fingered the top button on her nightgown. "So I guess I'll go contemplate serenity," she said with a sigh. She walked to the door and turned back to Sam. "I do look much better than Becky now, don't you think?"

"No one will confuse the two of you, that's for sure."

"Good," Allie answered, and then headed to the kitchen.

Sam jumped into a steaming hot shower to jolt herself awake and thought about the twins. If anything, they were in even worse shape than the previous summer. And it seemed that Mr. Jacobs just wasn't taking the situation seriously. Becky had been right about him dating up a storm. Since Sam had arrived, he'd gone out almost every night and, according to Becky, never with the same woman twice.

"What do you guys want for breakfast?" Sam asked when she got down to the kitchen.

"I already made some oatmeal," Allie said, getting a bowl from the cupboard.

"Barf city," Becky said, opening the refrigerator to peruse the contents. Apparently nothing appealed to her. "I'll just have toast," she decided.

Sam started the coffee and put some bread in the toaster. That was another change. The summer before, Mr. Jacobs had made sure that the twins ate a full breakfast, even though they were always screaming that they were on diets. This summer it seemed like he didn't pay any attention at all to what they ate, so Sam tried to.

"How about some yogurt with that," Sam suggested, "and some fruit?"

"No thanks," Becky said, getting the toast out of the toaster. "What I'd really like is a cigarette."

Sam turned on Becky. "Come on, you don't really smoke."

"Yes, I do," Becky answered blithely. "I just don't smoke around here, because Dad would have a coronary."

Well, at least that's one thing he's still sane about, Sam thought. She sat down next to Becky and looked her straight in the eye. "Listen to me. Smoking cigarettes is one of the stupidest things you can do in this world."

Becky just shrugged and buttered her toast. "What's the big deal?"

"The big deal," Sam said, "is cancer and a whole bunch of other diseases."

"Hey, when you gotta go, you gotta go!" Becky said, biting into her toast.

Sam couldn't believe how stupid Becky was acting. She looked over at Allie for support. Allie was quietly scooping oatmeal onto her spoon.

"Don't look at me," Allie said. "I told her it was stupid."

"Listen, I gotta run. I'm meeting my friends at the beach," Becky said, picking up her toast to take it with her. "The ones I have left since my sister turned into a religious freak, that is," she added pointedly, and ran upstairs to get her bathing suit.

"I'll pray for her," Allie said solemnly.

Someone should pray for me—I'm stuck in this loony bin, Sam thought as she sipped her first cup of coffee of the day.

Since both of the twins had plans, Sam had the morning off. After a run on the beach, she jogged back to the house to make lunch for the girls. The phone was ringing as she hit the front door.

"Jacobs residence," she answered.

"Hey, real formal!" Marina laughed. "I like it!"

"Oh, hi, Marina," Sam said. "What's up?"

"Well, I called my friend Delores this morning," Marina began. "She's a dancer, too—she works at the health club with me. Anyway, I asked her if she'd ever heard of this Show World International thing. She said they produce the show at the Mansion Hotel in Manhattan, and the one at the Sentry Hotel in Miami Beach."

"Tell me about them!" Sam asked with excitement.

"You mean you've never heard of those places?" Marina asked. "Well, the Mansion is this incredibly expensive new hotel in New York, and they have this Vegas-type revue running there. Same thing at the Sentry. Delores says she knows a girl in the Mansion show, and the girl is making tons of money!"

Sam had to sit down with the phone. "You're kidding," she breathed.

"Of course, she's been there a while," Marina continued. "I don't know if they start out at that high. But listen, this company is the real thing!"

"Yes!" Sam screamed, jumping up again.

"So I'm definitely doing this audition thing on Saturday," Marina concluded. "Are you in?"

"A football team of gorgeous guys couldn't keep me away . . . although they might make me late," Sam amended.

"I gotta run to the club," Marina said, "but I just wanted to let you know. We'll talk more about it tonight, okay?"

"Absolutely!" Sam agreed.

She hung up the phone and waltzed around the kitchen. "Big time, here I come!" she sang at the top of her lungs. *No, wait,* she said to herself. *I'm not going to let myself get too excited too soon. This is just an audition. There is no guarantee that Show World International will actually offer me a high-paying, glamorous job abroad as a dancer.*

But she couldn't help letting a small smile come to her lips. Maybe the next time Emma and Carrie started bugging her about what she was going to do in the fall, she'd be able to tell them.

"And I thought dancing at Disney World was hot stuff!" Sam scoffed out loud as she ran upstairs. "Ha!"

FIVE

"You're sure I look okay?" Sam asked
Marina anxiously as they got out of Mr.
Jacobs's car on Saturday.

"Sam, get a grip," Marina instructed.
They walked across the street to the dance
studio where the audition was being held.

Sam hadn't slept very well, she'd been so
excited about the audition. All night long
she had been thinking about what it would
be like to go abroad as a professional dancer.
The more she thought about it, the more she
wanted it to happen, and the more she wanted
it to happen, the more nervous she got about
the audition.

Still, she had to admit that things had
worked out so far almost as if she were
charmed. First of all, on Friday Dan Jacobs
had said he would be spending Saturday
afternoon at the beach with the twins even

before Sam had gotten a chance to ask for the time off. Second, he had volunteered to let Sam use his car—she hadn't even had to ask!

And then, just to put a capper on her good luck, Marina had loaned her the world's most excellent leotard. She'd just come by the Jacobses' house unexpectedly and dropped it off. It was black and hot pink, with high-cut legs. In the front it looked reasonably modest, but the back plunged . . . and plunged some more. Sam had twisted around in front of the mirror for an hour trying to decide if it looked awesome or slutty. She had finally decided it looked awesome—she hoped.

But now that she and Marina were actually about to go in to the audition, she wondered if she'd made a wise decision. Maybe it was too much. Marina didn't seem worried at all. On the other hand, Sam hadn't had a chance to see what her new friend was wearing—Marina had on a sweatshirt and jeans over her dance outfit, as did Sam.

Sam pushed open the door marked Dance Loft. Inside were about twenty girls in leotards. They were stretching against every surface in sight. To Sam they all looked gorgeous, perfect, and self-confident. Sam felt a lump of fear growing in her throat and turned toward Marina.

"No biggie," Marina said, seeing the fear etched on Sam's face. "I bet you can dance rings around all of them."

Sam smiled gratefully, and she and Marina made their way to the desk to pick up their applications.

"Height—five feet five inches," Marina said out loud with a groan as she filled out her application form. "Why God had to make me a short dancer, I'll never know," she said with a sigh.

"For the same reason he made me a flat-chested one, I guess," Sam said, filling out her own application.

"Not the same at all," Marina answered. "Dancers are supposed to be flat-chested."

"Yeah? Tell that to *them*," Sam said, indicating a group of four girls laughing together across the room. They were all tall, beautiful, and stacked.

"They probably can't walk and chew gum at the same time," Marina said, looking back down at her application.

"Hey, it says here you have to have a passport," Sam said. "Do you have a passport?"

"Yep," Marina answered. "You never know where you might end up going."

"Oh well, I guess I can get one . . . if they offer me a job, that is," Sam decided.

"I'm done," Marina said. "You ready to warm up?"

"Sure," Sam said, trying to sound much more blasé than she felt.

Marina added the applications to the pile on the table while Sam slipped out of her jeans and sweatshirt.

"Well, what do you think?" Sam asked nervously.

Marina grinned. "You look hot—hotter than hot, I swear!"

"Thanks," Sam said. "It was nice of you to loan it to me. But I keep thinking, if this is your second-best leotard, what does your first . . ."

Sam's words died on her lips. Marina had just stepped out of her jeans and sweatshirt, and Sam saw what her best leotard looked like. There stood Marina in glittery silver and flesh-colored mesh—more mesh than silver. The strips of silver managed to cover the minimum that had to be covered while giving the effect of almost total nudity. The mesh held the whole thing together. Two little strings tied each side of the leotard at her waist.

"*Wow* would be an understatement," Sam observed. "Where did you get that?"

"Oh, this old thing." Marina laughed. "Seriously, I picked it up in Vegas when I went to visit a friend who was in a show at the Sands. Isn't it great?"

"Awesome," Sam agreed. "I feel like Little Orphan Annie next to you."

"Hey, we're the two hottest girls in here," Marina told Sam, "and now everyone knows it."

The other girls in the waiting area were giving Marina and Sam the kind of envious looks that Sam had been giving them just a few minutes before.

"Yeah, we are," Sam agreed, throwing her wild hair back. "Let's warm up."

Sam and Marina found an empty spot and went through a stretching routine. As they warmed up, a bored-looking guy with bad skin called in a group of ten girls to audition. They came out after about twenty minutes, and then the next group was called in. Sam and Marina heard their names on the list and filed past the bored guy. Sam tried shooting him a smile—*it can't hurt*, she figured. But he just looked even more bored and rolled his eyes. Evidently he wasn't going to be any help at all.

"Girls, please line up behind the numbers on the floor so we can take a look at you," a

71

thin young woman with a British accent called out.

Across the front of the room, the numbers one through ten were written on pieces of paper. Marina shrugged and stepped behind number four. Sam stepped behind number five.

Facing them, behind a long table, were six people—four men and two women—silently judging them. Sam felt as self-conscious as if she were naked. She noticed that all down the line girls were beaming huge, fake Hollywood-type smiles at the judges, but none of the judges was beaming back.

Just then Sam's eye fell on Jack Germaine, the talent scout she and Marina had met at Bailey's. He smiled directly at her, and she smiled genuinely in return. That made her feel a little better.

"Okay, girls, turn sideways, please," came the British-accented voice again. The girls all turned.

"This is like being in a police lineup," Marina mumbled to Sam as she turned and sucked in her nonexistent gut.

"And a back view now, please," the woman intoned. The girls all obliged by turning to face the back wall.

"In Kansas you see this sort of thing when they're judging cattle at the state fair," Sam said, looking at the pale green wall. Marina barely stifled a laugh—it made both of them feel better.

"Delightful, girls. Now Tiffany, one of our choreographers, will put you through a few combinations. Tiffany?" The woman nodded in the direction of an Asian girl with hair past her waist.

"Hey, Tiffany is shorter than I am!" Marina whispered to Sam. "Maybe there's hope!"

"Okay, can everybody see me?" Tiffany said. "Stagger your spacing in the line, please."

Some girls moved forward and some moved back.

"We'll be doing eight combinations of eight today," Tiffany said. "I'll show you the whole thing first."

While they waited for the taped music to begin, Sam reviewed what Tiffany meant— that there would be eight different short routines of eight counts each, and put together they would form the entire routine.

"Five, six, seven, eight!" Tiffany counted, her arms outstretched in preparation. Tiffany whirled through the dance—it wasn't difficult so much as it was fast, and it had a lot of attitude. There was even a "free eight," which meant that for eight counts each girl could improvise whatever steps she wanted. When Tiffany finished, the group of auditioners burst into applause.

"All right, I'll break it down for you without the music," Tiffany said. "We start with a touch step to the right . . ."

Sam and Marina concentrated fiercely while Tiffany went through the routine, the auditioners copying her as she went along.

"We'll have you try it in groups of five," Tiffany said, stepping back.

"Gee, it's a lot easier if you do it in front of us," one girl said.

"Sorry," Tiffany said cheerfully. "You're on your own."

"We'll see numbers one through five first, please," the British woman said crisply.

"Why did I have to be in the first group?" Sam moaned under her breath. She knew the second group would have the added advantage of watching the combinations one more time.

"Five, six, seven, eight!" Tiffany counted off, and then Sam didn't have time to think anymore, only to dance. When she got to the third combination of eight, the one with the hip isolation off the beat, she knew she flubbed it a little, but that made her even more determined when it got to the free dancing. Sam went wild, and as she whirled around she noticed Marina was giving it her all, too.

Sam missed one more double kick, but finished big with just the right amount of leg extension and sexy attitude on the final beat. She was breathing hard, and when she turned her head, Marina winked at her. *Well, so far, so good,* Sam thought, relaxing.

The girls stepped back and let the next group of five do the same routine, and then they were all dismissed.

"Be sure you take an information packet on the way out," the British woman announced. "You'll receive a phone call within a week if we're interested in you."

"Well, how did we do?" Sam asked Marina as they put their jeans and sweatshirts on in the waiting area.

"Frankly, as far as I could tell, these girls were a poor excuse for dancers—present company excepted, of course."

"Meaning they wouldn't cut it in New York?" Sam asked, pulling her long hair out of the neck of her sweatshirt.

"Meaning they wouldn't cut it at a go-go

bar in Newark," Marina said. She held the door open for Sam.

"I don't know," Sam said as they crossed the street. "I thought that tall girl in the white leotard was good."

"Well, she was the only one," Marina said, "and she looked good only in comparison to the rest of them."

"So maybe that means we have a chance," Sam said, opening the car door.

"Maybe," Marina agreed. "But I figure they have tons of these regional auditions. There's no guarantee that they'll take even one person from here."

"I guess not," Sam said with a sigh. She started the car and backed out of the lot. "Listen, tell me something in all honesty, no bull, okay?"

"What?"

"Am I a good enough dancer to make it in New York?" Sam asked.

Marina twisted her long hair back into a ponytail and looked thoughtful. "Yes. And no," she finally said. "The yes part is that you've got talent, you really do. And the no part is that you've got no technique—you haven't studied enough. Talent without technique isn't enough in New York," Marina stated.

Sam turned toward the beach and sighed. "Yeah, I never really did apply myself to it. I mean, it always just came so easily to me. I'd even cut dance class for a date with a cute guy—"

"Well, that was stupid," Marina said flatly.

"I was a dumb high school kid, what did I know?" Sam said in her own defense. "Besides, I didn't grow up with this burning desire to be a dancer. I was just always really good at it, and I managed to get a college scholarship because of it, and . . . well, here I am!"

"I'll tell you the truth, Sam," Marina said as she pulled some dark sunglasses out of her purse. "With an attitude like that, you've got no shot at all. You have to be willing to sweat for it, hurt for it, want it so bad you can taste it."

Sam looked at Marina quickly and then back at the road. "Is that how you feel?" she asked Marina.

"You betcha," Marina said.

From the determined look on Marina's face, Sam knew she was telling the truth.

"Yeah, so what did this Tiffany chick look like?" Becky asked Sam. She was sitting on the edge of Sam's bed that night, absorbing every detail about Sam's dance audition.

Sam winced. "It's really uncool to call a woman a chick," she said.

"Oh please, Sam, get a life." Becky picked a nail file off Sam's dresser and started sawing at a chip. "What did this Tiffany *person* look like—is that better?"

"Much," Sam said with a grin. "Well, she was really tiny and in great shape, with black hair all the way down past her waist—"

"I think I should dye my hair black," Becky interrupted. "What do you think?"

"I think your hair is beautiful and you should leave it alone," Sam said, eyeing Becky's chestnut-brown waves, which, at the moment, were not gunked up with hair spray like they usually were.

"Do you think Allie has flipped her lid?" Becky asked Sam, changing the topic completely.

"Uh, no," Sam said. "I think—"

"Well, I do," Becky announced. "Honestly, I can't even stand sharing a room with her anymore."

"You never could," Sam reminded her.

"This is different," Becky said. "It's really weird. It's, like, the more conservative she gets, the wilder I get, and the wilder I get, the more conservative she gets."

"She's trying to find her own identity, I guess," Sam said, tucking her feet under her on the bed.

"That's what Dad says. I think she's just ticked because this guy we both were interested in liked me better. She's really pissing me off."

"She says the same thing about you," Sam told Becky. "Have you tried to talk about it instead of just screaming at each other?"

"I'd like to," Becky admitted, staring at Sam's bedspread. "I mean, it's kind of lonely now and everything. But every time I try to tell her, she just says she'll pray for me."

Sam sighed. "That's a tough one."

"Yeah," Becky agreed, flipping the nail file back onto the dresser. "It's like some science fiction movie—*Invasion of the Body Snatchers* or something. I really wish I could have my sister back."

"Maybe we could—" Sam began, but the phone rang, cutting her off. "Just a sec," she said, and padded into the hall.

"Jacobs residence," Sam said.

"Hey, beautiful, how you doin'?" came Presley's soft twang over the phone.

"Oh, hi, Pres," Sam said. She sounded a little cool and she knew it. But the memory of Pres staring after Diana De Witt's retreating figure had just come into her head.

"Listen, the Flirts are gonna be at the Play Café tonight," Pres said. "Think you can come by?"

"Mr. Jacobs is out tonight, so I'm stuck with the mon—I mean, the twins," Sam said, remembering that Becky could hear her.

"Too bad," Pres said. "Carrie's comin' by, and Emma and Kurt said they'd try to come, too."

"Maybe if Mr. Jacobs gets back at a reasonable hour," Sam mused. "He probably won't, though. He's into this new party-till-you-drop mentality."

"Yeah, those over-thirty guys can go all loony on you," Pres sympathized.

"Is that what happens when you're over thirty?" Sam said with a laugh.

"I don't know. You gonna marry some ole Kansas boy and have a bunch of babies?" Pres teased.

"Perish the thought," Sam said with a shudder. "I plan to be rich, famous, and lusted after by the great men of the world—and I doubt that you'll be among them," she added.

"You wound me, Sam, you really do," Pres said. "Well, how about if I ask you out on an actual date?"

"Sort of like Barbie and Ken?" Sam asked.

"Yes, you smartass," Pres said with a laugh. "Want to catch a movie Monday night?"

"Wow, you're asking me out two days in advance! You must be crazy about me," Sam said flirtatiously.

"Well, it's about time you got that message, sweet thing." Pres chuckled. "I'll pick you up about eight."

Becky stepped in front of Sam in the hall and looked at Sam critically as she hung up the phone. "You have the stupidest look on your face."

"Do I?" Sam asked. She was thinking about Pres. He really was *so* hot.

"How come you're always telling me not to act boy-crazy, and then a guy calls you and you get that stupid look on your face?" Becky asked.

"I'm nineteen and you're fourteen," Sam pointed out.

"Trust me," Becky snorted. "That moony look is just as silly-looking on you as it is on me."

Becky tossed her head and walked away to her room.

Well, Sam thought grudgingly, *I have to admit, every once in a while Becky is a really smart kid.*

Sam purged the moony look from her face and resolved to stay cool, calm, and collected about Pres.

At least for the moment.

SIX

Sam had just finished preparing the twins an enormous breakfast of scrambled eggs, grits, bacon, toast, and coffee when the telephone rang. Sam was pleased to see that they were both actually eating for once. But all interest in food ended as soon as they heard the ringing of the phone. Both Becky and Allie jumped up to get it.

"It's for me!" Becky yelped. "That really cute guy I met at the club on Saturday said he'd call me. That's him."

"Uh-uh, it's for me," said Allie, scrambling for the phone. "I'm expecting a call from this convent in California I wrote to last week. An article I read in the paper says they sometimes accept really young girls if they're completely unloved and neglected at home."

Becky beat Allie to the phone, however. Sam sat, exasperated, at the kitchen table. *It's not even ten o'clock*, she thought, *and I'm already totally exhausted by these two. Why couldn't they be the ages of the Hewitt kids?* Then she thought about what Becky and Allie must have been like at age eight, and the thought made her happy that they were teenagers. Sam knew that Dan Jacobs and his wife had split up when the girls were six. Rumor had it that she'd run off with a younger guy and hadn't been heard from since. The girls never brought it up, so Sam didn't either.

Becky's voice cut through the house like fingernails on a blackboard. "Oh, Saaa-aam! It's for you! Some guy."

Now, who would be calling me at this hour? Pres? No, he wouldn't even be awake yet. Oh, I bet it's that creep Taylor from the club. Okay, I'll answer the phone with a really croaky voice and pretend it's not me, Sam said to herself.

She got up and went to the phone. "Hello?" she croaked.

"Samantha Bridges?" an official-sounding voice on the other end of the line asked.

This doesn't sound like Taylor, she thought to herself. "Yes, this is she," she said in her normal voice. "Do I know you?"

"Ms. Bridges, my name is William Vanderbilt. I'm the director of talent placement for Show World International in New York City."

Sam's heart skipped a beat. "Really?" she managed to gulp out.

"Really," the smooth voice assured her. "Our scouts in Bangor were extremely impressed with your audition. They were unanimous in recommending that we offer you a position in our international dance company."

Yes! It's happening! It's really happening! Sam tried to contain herself, to act as professionally and coolly as she knew her friend Marina would. But she couldn't. When she spoke again, it was with a waver in her voice.

"A-as a professional dancer?"

"Yes, Ms. Bridges, as a professional dancer. Of course, should you elect to work with us, there's a three-month probationary period stipulated by your contract. During that time we may terminate you with no notice, so long as we provide you with return airfare to the stateside destination of your choice. However, if you pass your probation, and there's no reason to think that you would not, your contract would then extend for twelve months, renewable at our option."

"I see," Sam said, trying to sound adult. She knew there were questions she should be asking, but what? Suddenly, her mind was a complete blank. She shook her head, and a question finally came to her. "What is the pay?"

"The information packet we gave you in Bangor has the full details, Ms. Bridges. But briefly, we pay three hundred twenty-five dollars per week, plus housing, of course."

"And you fly me there, right?" Sam asked.

"Of course we fly you there," Mr. Vanderbilt said with amusement in his voice. "It would be such a tiresome bus ride."

Sam attempted a laugh, but it was difficult to do in a state of shock. "Right! Ha ha!"

"Give that back, you slimy slut-lizard!" Allie yelled at Becky in the kitchen.

Sam put her hand over the receiver. "Hey, kids, shut up!" she screeched. Sam cleared her throat and removed her hand from the mouthpiece. "Sorry about the interruption, Mr. Vanderbilt. This sounds . . . well, it sounds terrific! Where would I be working, and when would you want me to start?"

Sam could hear Mr. Vanderbilt shuffling some papers. "Ah, we have you slated to begin in either one week or one month, at your option. Your destination would be Japan."

Japan! Sam thought. *Wow. What would Marina do in this situation? Okay, I'll stall him for a bit while I figure out what to do.* "This sounds very interesting, Mr. Vanderbilt. But I need a couple of days to think it over. Can I call you on, say, Wednesday morning?" Sam asked.

"Make it by tomorrow afternoon, okay, Ms. Bridges?" Sam thought she heard a note of annoyance in Mr. Vanderbilt's voice.

"Fine, sir. And thank you very much."

"Thank you, too, Ms. Bridges. Good-bye." Mr. Vanderbilt hung up.

Sam went back to the kitchen, bursting to tell somebody her news, but all she found was a note—the twins had already left. *We went to the club*, the note said. *Dad said you should meet us for lunch. Allie's stopping at church on the way. See you later.* The food she had cooked was left congealing on the plates on the kitchen table.

I'll face that mess later, Sam thought, and went back to the telephone to call Marina.

Marina had also received a call from Mr.

Vanderbilt, and she had been offered the chance to go to Japan, too.

"I can't believe this! This is so awesome!" Sam screamed into the telephone. "We'll be going to Japan together!" She was so excited, she was practically bouncing around the room.

"It's the coolest," Marina agreed. "So listen, here's my plan. I'm gonna go right back to New York, pack my stuff, and be in Japan in a week or so."

"But what about your job at the Vertical Club?" Sam asked. "And Mrs. Bauersachs?"

"Frankly, I think Mr. Bauersachs has got eyes for me, and Mrs. Bauersachs is not digging it, if you catch my drift," Marina said.

"Can't you just talk to her?" Sam asked.

"Not about something like this," Marina said. "I'm the kid she never had only so long as I don't interfere with her happy, rich life, know what I mean?"

"That sucks," Sam said softly.

"Yeah, well, you win some, you lose some. This is really the best thing that could happen to me right now. This way she won't actually have to ask me to leave or anything. Anyway, I'm a dancer, not a lifeguard."

"Well, I'm going to wait for a month," Sam

said. "I've got to give the Jacobses notice, and a million other things."

"That's cool," Marina said, "so I'll see you in a few weeks."

Sam paced with the phone. "The whole thing just seems too good to be true," she said. "You're sure you've checked these guys out?"

"They are totally legit," Marina assured her. "I think you just got the break you've been looking for. It really can happen, you know."

"Yeah, I guess it really can," Sam agreed thoughtfully.

After she hung up, Sam knew she had to tell Emma and Carrie the news. *They will be so psyched for me*, she thought as she dialed Emma first.

"Hewitt residence, Emma Cresswell speaking."

"Hey, Emma, guess what?" Sam didn't even bother to say hello, she was so excited. "I just got a call from that dance company in New York, and they want me to go to Japan! And they want Marina, too!"

"Wow! That's fabulous, Sam," Emma said, her voice filled with genuine happiness for her friend. Then Emma paused. "But please don't forget what happened with Flash Hathaway last summer—"

"I knew you'd immediately bring his name up," Sam said. "This is absolutely nothing like that."

"As long as you're sure," Emma said.

"That's why I'm calling," Sam said. "I really want to talk to you and Carrie about it before I make my final decision. I told them I would let them know for sure by tomorrow afternoon. How about you, Carrie, and I meet at the pier later this afternoon, say, around two? We can take a walk, catch some rays, and still be home in time to take care of our kids for dinner."

Emma laughed. "It sounds like you have it all worked out, Sam. Let me clear it with Carrie and the Hewitts, and I'll call you right back. And congratulations. I always knew that you'd make it as a professional dancer."

The girls all got permission from their employers to take off a couple of hours in the afternoon. When Sam arrived at the pier, Emma and Carrie were already there. Carrie was wearing an old pair of cutoff jeans and a Yale T-shirt, while Emma, who would overdress to take out the garbage, had on white pleated pants with a black tank top and a big white hat.

"You look like something out of an ad for the Bahamas," Sam told her. Then she sighed happily. "Isn't it gorgeous out here?"

They decided they would walk to the end of the beach and back. The beach was practically deserted since the bulk of the summer residents hadn't arrived yet. It was almost high tide, the ocean had two-foot breakers on it, and the girls walked right along the waterline as they strolled. The only noise was from a couple of four-wheel-drive vehicles carrying surfcasting fishermen down the beach in search of the perfect spot.

"*This* is like an ad for the Bahamas," Carrie said to no one in particular. "Are you sure that you want to leave this to go dance in Japan? Why can't you go at the end of the summer?"

"They want me now," Sam said, stooping to pick up a flat stone and then skimming it across the waves.

"Hey, I never knew you could throw like that," Emma said.

"There's a lot of things you don't know about me," Sam said mysteriously, kicking sand ahead of her. "Like the fact that I'm going to come back from Japan a star."

"Sam," Carrie said, "I just want to be sure

that you asked all the right questions. You know that you're, well, somewhat impetuous sometimes. On the other hand, this may be a really great chance for you."

Sam waved to three cute guys driving by in a Jeep with fishing rods lashed to the side. "I looked at everything, you guys. I reread the literature they gave me at the audition, asked about my contract, found out what the pay is—everything. I mean it!" she finished emphatically.

"Whoa, Sam." Carrie tugged on her friend's arm. "I said I thought that this might be a great opportunity for you. I'm just making sure that you're doing the right thing."

"Right," said Emma. "We're your friends. We're just watching out for you."

"Look," Sam said, turning to the two of them, "I've already got two parents. I don't need two more."

They continued walking down the beach in silence. Finally, Sam turned back to her friends.

"I'm sorry. It's just that my parents sometimes treat me like I can't make my own decisions, like I'm still a child, and I'm not. I was thinking about the phone call that I have to make to tell them about this," Sam said. "It's not exactly something that I'm looking forward to doing."

"What do you think is going to happen?" Emma asked as they approached a group of fishermen standing knee-deep in the ocean. "Do you think they'll hate the idea of you going?"

"I don't *think* they'll hate it. I *know* they'll hate it," Sam said with a bitter little laugh.

"Well, don't worry," Carrie said, smiling. "If it's what you want to do, you know we'll back you one hundred percent."

"Thanks, you guys," Sam said. "I really appreciate—hey, look out there!" Sam was pointing wildly to the ocean, about fifty yards offshore. The water was boiling madly; flocks of seagulls were flying close to the surface and starting to wheel and dive toward the water. The fishermen down the beach splashed up after them.

"Bluefish! Big school of blues!" one of the hip-booted fishermen yelled out as he passed. The girls watched in amazement as a fisherman let fly with a spectacular cast while he was still at a dead run, flinging a lure right into the middle of the boiling ocean. He started reeling in the line, twitching the tip of his rod to make the lure jerk in the water. Suddenly, something grabbed his lure, making the rod bend nearly double.

"Wow!" Sam exclaimed. "That is seriously outrageous. He must have a huge fish!"

"I've done that," Emma said, watching.

"You've done *everything*," Sam said, laughing.

"No, it's true," Emma said. "One time I was with my parents on Cape Cod during a bluefish run, and one of their friends took me out surfcasting. I think what we're watching is a surf fisherman's dream. That water looks like it's boiling because there's a huge school of bluefish feeding on a school of small baitfish near the surface. That's what makes the water churn like that."

"Are bluefish really blue?" Carrie asked curiously.

"Not until they get hauled out of the water. Then they're really unhappy!" Sam chortled. "Look! That guy just got his out. Let's go see it!"

The girls rushed over to where the fisherman was pulling a big blue by the tail up out of the water. It was sleek and steel-gray. It was still thrashing.

"Are those good to eat?" Sam asked the guy.

"You bet, especially when they're fresh," said the fisherman. "Want to try landing one?"

"Uh, no thanks," Sam said, looking quickly at her nails and imagining what fighting a bluefish might do to them. "Maybe another time."

"Okay," said the fisherman, and he waded back into the ocean.

The girls walked back to the pier, buzzing excitedly about what they had just watched. They knew this was a part of Sunset Island life that many people never got a chance to see.

Sam spent the rest of the day preparing dinner for Becky and Allie and keeping an eye on them, since Mr. Jacobs was off on yet another of his dates. The twins were asleep by ten-thirty—a rarity in the Jacobses' house—and Sam watched the clock anxiously until eleven. She had resolved to call her folks to tell them about Japan when the phone rates went down.

She dialed Junction at eleven-fifteen. It was an hour earlier there. Sam nibbled nervously on potato chips as she dialed.

"Hello, Mom? Hi, it's me, Sam," she said when her mother answered.

"Samantha, this is an unexpected surprise! How nice of you to call. Is everything all right?" There was a note of concern in her mother's voice.

"Everything's fine, Mom. Listen, can you get Dad on the extension? I have some good news, and I want to tell you both at the same time, okay?"

When her father got on the phone, Sam wasted little time. She bit her lip, and with as much enthusiasm as she could muster, she told them the whole story about Show World International and the offer to go to Japan. "So, isn't that great?" she concluded. "My big break!"

Sam didn't expect a very warm response from her folks, and she didn't get one. There was silence on the other end of the line.

"Hello?" Sam said. "Anyone there?"

"We're here," her dad finally said evenly.

"Look, Mom, Dad," Sam said earnestly, "this is the kind of thing I've been training to do my whole life."

"Training?" her mother repeated. "I used to have to beg you to go to dance class!"

"Well, I'm more serious about it now," Sam said. "You've been telling me forever that I have to get serious about something, and I finally did!"

"What about college, Sam?" her dad asked.

"Why should I go back to college to learn how to be a dancer when I could go to Japan and actually *be* a dancer?"

"But, Sam, how do you know it's going to work out?" Mrs. Bridges asked. "What if you get there and you hate it? Your scholarship to Kansas State won't wait forever."

"How do you know anything about the future?" Sam shot back hotly. "You just don't want me to go because you've always wanted me to go to school."

"That's not true, Sam," her father said. "We just want to make sure that you do the right thing."

"Who knows better what's the right thing for me, you or me?" Sam reasoned.

"Sometimes I wonder," Mr. Bridges murmured.

"That is so unfair, Dad," Sam fumed. She took a deep breath. She *hated* fighting with her parents. "Look, this is a decision I'm old enough to make for myself. What I need is for you to send me my birth certificate so I can apply for a passport."

There was more silence from the Kansas end of the phone.

"Did you hear me?" Sam asked. "I need my birth certificate."

Sam's mother said brightly to her father, "Dear, you have it in the safe-deposit box at the bank in Kansas City, don't you? It'll be a few days before you'll have a chance to go pick it up, won't it?" Her father agreed. Sam thought something sounded odd about the whole exchange, though.

"Look," Sam said, "if it's at all possible, I need it by Friday. The producers said they can take care of a lot of the paperwork for me if I get it to them by then."

Sam's father spoke up. "I'll . . . I'll try to do that," he agreed in a strange tone of voice. "I need to talk to your mother now, Sam. Bye." And he hung up quickly. Her mother hung up, too. Sam was left there holding the phone.

There's something I missed here, Sam thought. And though she lay awake thinking until one in the morning, she couldn't for the life of her figure out what it was.

SEVEN

"Becky, you really should pull your skirt down," Allie admonished. "It's unseemly."

It was the next day, and Sam was taking Becky and Allie to lunch at the Play Café. Emma had a few hours off because Jane and Jeff Hewitt were taking their kids out on their boat, so she was meeting Sam and the twins for lunch.

"Puh-leeze," Becky said, rolling her eyes, "give me a break with that stuff."

The three crossed the street, and Sam pushed open the door to the café.

"I only tell you out of love," Allie said primly, fingering the lace collar on her pristine white blouse.

Becky snorted and moved closer to Sam. "Listen, I can't stand having the world know I'm even related to her, much less her twin.

Could you just tell everyone that we're a pair of identical strangers?"

"I wish you two would talk to each other about this," Sam said as she scanned the café for Emma. "I guess she's not here yet. Let's get a table."

As they settled into a booth for four, Becky nudged Sam in the ribs. "Hey, look over there!" she cried, pointing to a couple and their teenage son who had just walked into the café. "That's that guy, Randy, who was flirting with me at the pool yesterday!"

Sam looked behind her and saw a cute guy of about sixteen walking to a table with a blond-haired woman and a dark-haired man who looked like an older version of the boy.

"Want to go say hello?" Sam asked.

"Are you kidding?" Becky hissed. "His *parents* are there!"

"They're parents, not lepers," Allie said loftily.

"Oh, come on, look at his father," Becky said. "He's wearing black stretch knee socks with shorts and sandals. If I go over there to talk to Randy, he will be humiliated for life."

Sam turned around again to look at Randy's father's outfit. Becky was right—he really did have on black stretch nylon knee socks with sandals and baggy bermuda shorts. He also had on a Hawaiian print shirt. Sam winced.

"Judge not, lest ye be judged," Allie lectured, wagging a finger at her sister. Then she turned around to look at Randy's father's outfit, and even *she* had to wince. "Well, maybe he's blind," she added lamely.

"I'm telling you, parents can be so embarrassing," Becky said, shaking her head. "They can, like, ruin your life." She stole another peek at Randy's father and shuddered. "I can't wait until I'm eighteen and free."

"That's not exactly how it works," Sam said ruefully, thinking about her own situation.

Just then the door opened and Emma walked serenely across the room.

She looks like a queen entering a palace, Sam thought, watching Emma. *How does she always manage to look so calm and controlled?*

"Sorry I'm a few minutes late," Emma acknowledged, sliding into the booth next to Allie. "I was on the phone with Kurt."

Becky gave Emma a wistful look. "It must be awesome, having a boyfriend that hot."

"It's pretty terrific," Emma agreed with a small smile.

"Hi, I'm Sally, and I'll be your waitress," came a flat Midwestern voice. "They make me say that," she added. "You guys need menus?" Sam looked up . . . and up, at a new waitress, one of the tallest, thinnest girls she had ever seen. Sally had brown hair pulled back into a limp ponytail and huge green eyes that peered down at them from behind thick glasses.

"You must be new," Sam said.

"I'm Ken Miner's niece," Sally said. "Lucky me, huh?" she added in a voice that implied she was anything but.

"Actually, we know the menu by heart," Emma said in her cultured voice. "I'll have the spinach salad."

"Yuck," Sally said matter-of-factly, but she wrote it down.

"I'll have the fruit salad with plain yogurt," Allie said.

"Double yuck," Sally said. "Next?"

"We're both having cheeseburger deluxes," Sam said, ordering for Becky, too. She wondered what Sally's reaction would be.

"Good choice," Sally said.

"With extra fries and extra cheese," Becky added. It was one of her I-don't-care-what-I-eat days, as opposed to her I'm-too-fat-I-can't-eat-anything days.

"With a double chocolate shake," Sam added, almost just so she could hear Sally's response.

"Now there's an order!" Sally said, nodding enthusiastically.

"Excuse me, but do you have something against healthy food?" Emma asked with amusement.

"Well, it's like this," Sally said. "The doctor said I needed to gain twenty pounds. So my mother made me go see this hypnotist, who put me under and gave me the post-hypnotic suggestion that I would like only fattening foods. He said that when I even *thought* about eating low-calorie foods, it would be like thinking about eating dirt."

"Wow, I guess it worked," Becky marveled.

"Yeah, I guess," Sally agreed. "But now Ken says that he's getting too many complaints about me commenting on people's food orders. I just can't win!" Sally shrugged and headed for the kitchen.

"Just another example of how parents can mess up your life," Becky said knowingly.

"Speaking of parents," Sam said to Emma, pushing her curls out of her face, "I had that little talk with the parental units last night."

"Talk about what?" Allie asked instantly.

Sam gave Emma a meaningful look. She wasn't about to tell the twins about her job offer to dance in Japan until she had given notice to their father, and that wouldn't happen until later in the day.

"About . . . something I asked them to send me," Sam said.

"What?" Allie asked.

"Just some little thing," Sam hedged.

"Tell us," Allie said. "We always tell you."

"Isn't there something in the Bible about minding your own business?" Sam asked Allie sweetly, a fake smile plastered on her face.

"Forget it, then. I'm not even interested," Allie said in a huff. "I'm going for a walk to contemplate the sins of the world." Allie got up from the booth and headed for the door.

"You just didn't want to tell her because she's gone to la-la land, but you'll tell me, right?" Becky asked hopefully.

"Wrong," Sam replied.

"Figures," Becky snorted. "I'm gonna go play video games."

"Maybe we should have shelved this conversation until later," Emma said after Becky was out of earshot. "After all, you *are* supposed to be working."

"Even getting rid of them is work," Sam said with a shrug.

"So what did your parents say about your taking the job?" Emma asked. "Was it horrible?"

"Worse," Sam said. "They were mondo bizarro about it. First they gave me all the usual blah-blah-blah about how I should be in college—"

"Well, you expected that," Emma said.

"But then they didn't even want to send me my birth certificate so that I can get a passport," Sam continued grimly. "I mean, how controlling can you get?"

"They just want to make sure you're doing the right thing," Emma said softly. "They love you."

"This isn't about love," Sam said firmly. "It's about control. My parents think that just because they gave birth to me, they have a right to control my life."

"Maybe if you proved to them how thoroughly you've checked out the company you'd be working for . . ." Emma suggested.

Sam sat back and folded her arms in anger. "What am I, guilty until proven innocent? Stupid until proven intelligent? What about them having a little faith in their daughter and treating me like a grownup?"

Emma nodded thoughtfully. Sam guessed that she really didn't feel like she was one to give advice on parents. Her relationship with each of her parents was terrible. "Listen, I do understand how you feel," Emma agreed earnestly. "I'm on your side, honest."

"Thanks," Sam said, somewhat mollified.

"But still," Emma continued, "if you want to get anywhere with them, you may have to take a less—oh, I don't know—combative approach."

"It's just that they make me so mad," Sam fumed.

"Yes, well, join the club," Emma said ruefully.

"Here's your dirt—I mean lunch," Sally said, gingerly depositing Emma's spinach salad in front of her. She put the rest of the plates in the appropriate places. "There are four different kinds of homemade pie for dessert!" Sally added enthusiastically as she headed back to the kitchen.

"Good timing!" Becky chirped, sliding into the booth and starting in on her food.

"I'm back," Allie announced, walking in at almost the same moment. "I hope you enjoyed your *secret* conversation."

Sam bit back a rejoinder and picked up her cheeseburger. Waving good-bye to the twins in a month was going to be one big, fat relief.

"So, that's pretty much it," Sam said as she finished telling Dan Jacobs why she was giving notice.

It was that evening, and Sam was all ready for her date with Pres. She and Mr. Jacobs were in the den. He had just returned from the gym and seemed like he was in a great mood. *No time like the present*, Sam had told herself, and plunged into her story.

"Well, I'm not sure what to say," Mr. Jacobs said, his hands dangling between his knees. "I guess one part of me is happy for you, but I'm really disappointed that you'll be leaving us."

"Me, too," Sam said, and at that particular moment she almost meant it.

"And you'd be leaving when, exactly?" he asked.

"In about four weeks," Sam answered. "I don't have an exact date yet."

"Are your parents excited for you?"

"No," Sam said bluntly. "In fact, we had a huge fight about it."

"Big mistake," her employer said, shaking his head. "I'll tell you, I learned my lesson with the twins. I used to watch over them like a hawk, remember?"

Sam nodded. *Who could forget?* she thought.

"But lately I've been taking a more live-and-let-live kind of attitude," he explained. "Hey, I'm not them and they're not me, right? It's a big improvement, don't you think?"

Sam thought about the current identity crisis the twins were going through. Frankly, she thought they were both a psychological mess, but she wasn't about to tell their father that.

"Well, it's . . . an interesting approach," Sam said cautiously.

"I guess I'll have to contact the National Au Pair Society about your replacement," Mr. Jacobs said thoughtfully.

"Yeah, I guess," Sam said. She felt a weird little *ping* in the area of her heart. *Your replacement*—she hated the way that sounded. "I guess that will be pretty easy, huh?" she added.

"To hire somebody, yes," Mr. Jacobs said. "To replace you, no."

A flush of pleasure came to Sam's face. "It's nice to know I'm appreciated," she said.

Mr. Jacobs looked at her. "As I've said

before, you've made a big difference in Becky and Allie's lives. I really hate to see you go."

"Sam, Pres is here," Becky said, appearing in the doorway. "He is so *fine!* I still can't believe he's going out with you."

Allie sidled up next to her. "What, do you expect him to go out with a gorilla like you?"

"Very funny," Becky shot back. "Who are you supposed to be, the patron saint of girls who can't get dates?"

Sam gave Mr. Jacobs a sickly smile. If she had made such a big difference in the twins' lives, it evidently wasn't in their manners.

Sam found Pres in the front hall admiring a photograph of the twins that hung above a small antique table.

"Hey, sweetheart," Pres drawled, turning to Sam. "You're lookin' real pretty." He appreciatively took in her faded jeans, red cowboy boots, and off-the-shoulder midriff-baring white cotton top.

"I'd fill that top out better than she would!" came a faceless voice from the hall. Then Becky popped her head around the corner and threw Pres a flirtatious look.

"Sweetheart, a lady never talks about her assets," he said softly. "She doesn't need to."

For once Becky couldn't come up with a

retort, and Sam and Pres made it out of the house without further delay.

"Doesn't her daddy say anything to her when she behaves like that?" Pres asked Sam when they got outside.

"He's into a hands-off attitude this summer," Sam said with a sigh.

"Well, they seem like two sweet but real messed-up little girls to me," Pres observed.

Sam laughed. "Watch out. They'd kill you for calling them little girls." Sam noticed the gleaming black Honda motorcycle parked in the driveway. "Cool! Did you rent it for the day or borrow it from one of your friends?" she asked.

"Actually, I bought it," Pres said sheepishly. "I was spending so much money renting 'em, I decided I might as well get my own."

"Well, it's a beauty," Sam said, admiring it.

"Yeah, so are the payments," Pres said ruefully, handing Sam a helmet.

The feel of the wind in her face and her arms around Pres's muscled torso were fabulous. Sam leaned her face into his jean-jacketed back. He even smelled good.

"We could just keep on ridin'!" Pres called back to her. "I could get used to feelin' you pressed up against me like that."

"Movies," Sam directed with a laugh. "We're going to the movies."

"Your wish is my command," Pres drawled, and turned the corner toward the island's only movie theater.

"A line," Sam sighed after they'd parked the bike and turned the corner onto the block where the theater was located. "Figures."

"Hey, stand behind me, wrap those luscious arms around me, and we'll just pretend we're still on the bike, how's that?" Pres said, pulling Sam's arms around him from behind.

Sam laughed and obliged. Then Pres turned around so that he was facing her. Her arms were still around him.

"That's even better," Pres murmured in a low voice.

"I'm not complaining," Sam said, looking up into his eyes.

"I sincerely missed you," Pres said, lifting a strand of hair off Sam's cheek.

"Especially during that long, frigid Maine winter, right?" Sam teased.

"Dang, girl, there's just something about you. . . ." Pres said.

"Well, if it isn't my favorite Tennessee mountain man," came a low, sexy voice from behind Sam. She turned around and groaned. It was Diana De Witt.

Diana pretended she had just noticed

Sam. "Oh, he's with you," she said disdainfully. "Well, I suppose everyone is entitled to the occasional lapse in good taste."

"Oh, hi, Diana," Sam said. "Are you waiting to see the horror movie, or are you starring in it?"

Diana laughed gaily. "I just love those clever little comebacks of yours! Actually, I'm with someone."

"Me," came a male voice from behind her. "I finally found a place to park."

It was Taylor, the guy who had flirted with Sam at Bailey's, the guy who was supposed to be pining away for someone named Wendy.

"Nice to see you again, Taylor," Sam said, choking back a laugh.

Taylor gave her a quizzical look. "Didn't we meet on the beach or something?"

Sam was taken aback. Guys usually remembered who she was and where they had met her. "Bailey's? Dancing? You told me all about Wendy, the love of your life?" Sam added maliciously.

"Oh yeah," Taylor said. "Well, I'm not thinking about Wendy anymore." He pulled Diana close.

"Evidently not," Sam said.

"We have to go get in line," Diana said.

She gave Pres a smoldering look. "Do you know where I live?" she asked him.

"You rented that white house by the Popes?" he asked.

"Smart boy," she purred. "Don't be a stranger," she added as she turned. "It gets lonely there at night."

"She is loathsome, disgusting, obnoxious, pitiful," Sam ranted.

"But how do you really feel?" Pres laughed.

"I'm serious, Pres," Sam fumed. "Do you know that at the end of last summer she seduced Emma's boyfriend just to prove she could get him? It broke Emma's heart."

"Aw, she's just flirtin' around," Pres said. "She's harmless."

They both turned around to look at harmless Diana, who was farther down the movie line. Diana caught Pres's eye and held it. Slowly and deliberately, she touched the tip of her tongue to her upper lip, smiled, and turned away.

"I may throw up," Sam said.

"I think she's a hoot," Pres opined. He was still staring at Diana's back.

Sam stifled an angry retort. The last thing she wanted to do was play stupid games with Diana De Witt.

The sooner I get off this island, the better, she vowed.

EIGHT

Sam and Becky were already lolling on the beach in the noonday sun when Carrie arrived with Graham Perry Templeton's thirteen-year-old son Ian in tow. Allie Jacobs had told Sam that she was going to sit by herself back by the dunes. That was exactly what she was doing, barely in sight of the others.

"What are you daydreaming about, Sam?" Carrie said to her friend with a smile as they approached. "And nice swimsuit—I wish I could get away with wearing something like that," she added wistfully. Sam had on a shocking pink maillot cut almost indecently high on the sides, decorated with a huge exclamation mark on the front. "If I wore that, the exclamation mark would look like a aerial photograph of the Rocky Mountains! Hi, Becky."

Sam and Becky both laughed. "I'd be happy to trade this exclamation mark for a bit of what would make those mountains, Carrie," Sam said with a grin. Then she noticed Ian blushing. "Girl talk, Ian," she said to him. "Do you know Becky Jacobs?"

"I've seen you around," Ian said to Becky. He was a cute, slender boy with long blond hair, and he looked a lot like his famous rock star father. Sam could still not believe Carrie's luck in being selected as the au pair for the world-renowned rocker Graham Perry Templeton, who under the stage name Graham Perry had played on the same bill as the Rolling Stones. He'd even had Rod Stewart open a show for *him*, but Carrie seemed to take the whole thing in stride. *Carrie takes everything in stride*, Sam thought.

Becky looked at Ian superciliously. She had on one of her patented nothing bikinis, and Ian was staring right at her top. "How old are you, actually?" Becky asked.

"Thirteen," Ian said, fidgeting a bit.

"I'm fourteen," Becky said, as if that ended the discussion. She turned back to the magazine she was reading.

"Do you guys want something to drink?" Sam asked, motioning to a cooler on the sand.

"Sure," said Carrie and Ian at the same time, and they laughed as they stretched out on the sand near Becky and Sam.

Sam stared out at the ocean as she sipped a soda. It was a very warm day, with not a cloud in the sky, but a strong wind gusted up at regular intervals. Windblown grains of sand dusted them from time to time, and the seagulls and sandpipers all were standing on the sand, their backs to the wind.

Sam was just about to fall asleep in the sun when she heard Ian speak.

"Hey, Becky," he said, "did you know that I have my own band at prep school?"

"Hmmm?" grunted Becky, uninterested.

"Yeah," Ian continued, sitting up. "It's called Lord Whitehead and the Zit Men. We got bummed out with current rock, we hate rap, and nobody plays that country crap, so we decided to focus on industrial music," he said proudly.

"Oh, I can hardly wait to hear what that is," Becky said, turning the page of her magazine.

"I'd like to know," Sam said, genuinely curious. She could see that even Becky was looking at Ian out of the corner of her eye. After all, he might be only thirteen, but his father *was* Graham Perry.

117

"Well, we don't exactly play instruments," Ian said. "We figure that's part of the problem with modern music. We do have a drum machine, but that's not really an instrument. It's more like a noisy video game."

Becky spoke up. "So what do the Zit Men do onstage? Bang tubes of Clearasil together and sing the lyrics from Stridex advertisements?"

Sam chortled, and even Carrie had trouble controlling her laughter.

"Not exactly," Ian said seriously. "Basically what we do is take the insides of washing machines, clothes dryers, and toasters, and then bang different kinds of sticks and brushes against them. Very industrial-sounding. We're sort of famous in our own way."

"I'll bet!" Becky said. "Hey, Allie!" she yelled. "C'mere. You gotta talk to this guy. He's right up your alley."

Sam and Carrie watched a white-draped figure rise from the dunes and make her way slowly toward them, like a North African desert ghost.

"Yes, Rebecca?" Allie said serenely when she got close to them.

"This is Ian Templeton. I think you and he have a lot in common," Becky said with a glint in her eye.

"You listen to industrial music?" Ian asked eagerly.

"I listen to madrigals and Gregorian chants," Allie said.

"I'm going for a swim," Carrie announced. "Want to come, Sam?"

The two of them ran toward the ocean without looking back, splashed into the cold waves, dunked their heads underwater, and came up snorting with laughter.

"Industrial music! Madrigals! Lord Whitehead and the Zit Men! Allie dressed like she just stepped out of some subtitled movie! Help me!" Sam screamed in a high voice, "I can't take it anymore! Japan, here I come!" she said. She dove back under the water and came back up behind Carrie. "Boo!" she yelled, making Carrie jump.

"Do you know when you're leaving yet?" Carrie asked.

"Well, I can't leave until I show the company a valid passport," Sam reminded Carrie. "And I can't get a passport until I have my birth certificate. I don't even know if my parental units mailed it yet."

"You could call again and ask," Carrie suggested reasonably.

"Yeah, I could," Sam agreed, floating on her back. "I just hate having to hear all that negativity from them again."

"Yeah, I hate fighting with my parents, too," Carrie sympathized.

"From what I've heard, you hardly ever do fight with them—lucky you," Sam added. She splashed to a standing position. "You want to know what I really think? I think they're not rushing to send it because they don't want me to take this job. They think that if the certificate doesn't come, then I won't really be able to go, or that something will come up that will make me want to stay here. Boy, have they got that wrong," Sam said with a touch of anger in her voice.

"Let's get out of the water," Carrie said. "I'm getting cold. I bet it isn't any warmer than sixty-something degrees in here. What I think you need to do," she went on, "is call them and level with them. As a person. Adult to adult. If you treat them like grown-ups and not like your parents, maybe they'll treat you the same way."

Sam shrugged as she walked up the beach. *I'm willing to try it*, she thought, *but since when do parents act like grownups?*

When Sam and Carrie got back to the twins and Ian, they found Billy Sampson sitting with them.

"Hey! Nice surprise!" Carrie said, grinning from ear to ear.

"Ian and I were just talking about whether you can get better sound from a Maytag or a Kelvinator," Billy said with a wink. "I was jogging on the beach, saw you guys in the water, and just had to wait for you to come out."

Carrie flopped down in Billy's arms. "Whoa, girl, you're all wet," Billy said to her. "Let me dry you off." Sam watched a little jealously as Billy sensuously toweled off Carrie's back and legs. *He's clearly crazy about her*, she thought wistfully. *Why can't someone be crazy about me who I want to be crazy back to?* she thought. *Hey!* said another voice in her head. *What about Danny, pining away for you back at Disney World? What about Pres, right here on the island? Maybe that isn't really what you want, after all.* . . . Sam gave herself a mental shake. She didn't want to think about guys at all. She wanted to think about Japan and dancing and great adventures. For once, guys could wait.

After an early dinner at the Jacobses' house, Mr. Jacobs took Becky and Allie to a movie. Sam thought he must be feeling guilty for going out on dates so often. He invited Sam to go along, but she said she was tired and just wanted to rest before a big going-away party that was planned for Marina Mazzetti at the Play Café later that night. Actually, she just wanted them all out of the house for what she thought would be one heavy telephone rap about Japan with her parents.

Sam dialed Kansas right after the Jacobses left for the movies. *I've got my nerve up for this*, she thought, *so it's now or never. Be cool, Sam*, she told herself. *Talk with them adult to adult*.

"Hello?"

Sam immediately recognized the voice of her younger sister, Ruth Ann. Seventeen-year-old Ruth Ann was as different in temperament and attitude from Sam as she could possibly be. When Sam and Ruth Ann were kids, Sam would have gladly murdered her sister and blamed it on some passing maniac. Things had gotten better as the two girls got older, but they still didn't understand each other at all. For example, Ruth Ann actually paid attention in math class, was a National Merit Scholarship semifinalist, was on the high school chess team, and planned to go to medical school. Sometimes Sam wondered how they could possibly have the same parents, they were that different.

"Ruth Ann? Hi, it's Sam!"

"Hi, Samantha! How's everything?" Ruth Ann asked.

Sam winced. She hated being called Samantha, and Ruth Ann knew it. "Oh, just fine, *Ruthie*," Sam said pointedly.

"Sorry." Ruth Ann laughed. "Hey, I heard Mom and Dad talking about some job offer that you got. Congratulations!"

Well, at least my folks are actually talking about me, Sam thought. *The big question is, what are they saying?*

"Thanks. The job sounds pretty cool. This big promoter in New York City came up here to hold auditions, and they picked me out of a huge group of girls to join their international dance company."

"That's what I heard," Ruth Ann said. "Are you going to be away a long time? Mom and Dad will miss you."

"Well, they haven't seen me that much recently, anyway," Sam pointed out. "It'll happen to you, too, once you're out of high school."

"Oh, no," Ruth Ann said. "I'm going to do my undergraduate work at Kansas State, and then do medical school there, too. I've got it all worked out."

Great, Sam thought. *She's completely programmed and she's barely seventeen years old.*

"Listen," Sam said, "are Mom and Dad around? I really have to talk to them. They were supposed to send me my birth certificate so that I can get a passport, and if it doesn't arrive here by the day after tomorrow, I'm dead meat."

"They went to the midget car races over in Colby. They won't be back till late," Ruth Ann said.

"Oh, that's just great," Sam groaned.

"Hey, wait," Ruth Ann said, "I think I saw your birth certificate on Dad's dresser. There was some official-looking envelope. Yes, I'm sure it's there."

"Ruth Ann, can you send it to me?" Sam asked eagerly. "It would save Dad a chore."

"Sure," Ruth Ann told her sister. "Tell you what, there's a new Package Express store that opened downtown. I'll take it there now and you can have it tomorrow. How's that?"

"Will they be open this late?" Sam asked doubtfully.

"I think so."

"Thanks a zillion, Ruth Ann. Do it right away, okay? My address is on the refrigerator, I think. Tell Mom and Dad hi. I miss you. Bye!"

Sam hung up with a sigh of relief. She'd have her birth certificate in time. *Nothing can stop me now*, she thought.

Sam changed clothes and watched TV until the Jacobses returned home from the movies. She'd put on a very sexy Nashville-looking outfit—a cotton shirt with epaulets and rhinestone buttons, a blue denim mini-skirt, and her trademark cowboy boots. To this she had added a white cowboy hat that made her look even taller than her normal five feet ten inches. Even Mr. Jacobs said she looked sensational before she left for Marina's party.

When she got to the Play Café, the party was already in full swing. Word that she and Marina had been selected by Show World International to go to Japan had spread like wildfire around the island, and it seemed like everyone between the ages of sixteen and twenty-five was at the party. Even though Marina Mazzetti had been on the island for only a few days, her self-assurance and street-smart ways had made her very popular.

As Sam walked into the Play Café a small, nerdy-looking guy came up to her. It was Howie Lawrence, a very nice, very rich, very enthusiastic, and not very attractive guy who had the hots for Carrie. Carrie liked him, but only as a friend, and Howie seemed to think that maybe the way to

Carrie's heart was through her friends Sam and Emma.

"Hi, Sam! Long time no see. Great party. Everyone's here," Howie said, reaching up to kiss Sam on the cheek.

Sam pecked back at the air. "Hi, Howie. How's your pool game doing this summer?"

"I'm hoping I can talk Carrie into giving me some pointers," Howie said with a grin. "I was talking to Carrie before, but then she disappeared. Can I get you a drink?"

"No thanks, Howie," Sam said. "I need to go find Carrie."

"Well," said Howie, looking over Sam's shoulder toward the ladies' room, "she went in that direction. If you see her, tell her I'm looking for her, too."

"Sure thing," said Sam, who had spotted Pres standing near the jukebox. She started to walk over to him. But then she stopped. Next to him, practically leaning on him, was none other than Diana De Witt. She had on a tight red spandex top and a silk sarong-style miniskirt, and all of a sudden Sam felt like she had made the wrong wardrobe choice.

Sam was just close enough to hear what Diana was saying to Pres over the incessant beat of rock music.

"I think it's so *won*-derful that you come from the South," Diana said, running her hands up and down Pres's biceps. "Southern men are such . . . passionate gentlemen!"

I think I'm gonna barf, Sam thought. She stood there watching Diana in action. What was it with her? Had she really developed a sudden interest in Pres, or was she just determined to work her way through all of her enemies' boyfriends?

I'm not going to roll over and play dead like Emma did last summer, that's for sure, Sam told herself. Suddenly it didn't matter that Sam wasn't even sure she wanted Pres. She wasn't sure what she wanted—except that she was determined to beat Diana at her own game.

Time for one heavy-duty reprisal, Sam thought, lifting her chin and narrowing her eyes. *Call out the B-52s!*

Sam scanned the Play Café and saw Taylor standing not more than ten feet away from Pres and Diana. *Okay, swallow your dignity. You're doing this for a reason*, she said to herself. *It doesn't matter that this guy is a creep. What matters is that Pres sees you.*

A moment later, Taylor was surprised by a woman putting her hands over his eyes

127

from behind and whispering "Guess who?" in his ear. He turned with a smile to find Sam gazing at him.

"Hey, I'm so glad you're here," he said to her, looking her right in the eye. "I've been thinking about you ever since I saw you at the movies."

Right, Sam thought. *At the movies you didn't even remember where you'd met me, and you were drooling all over Diana.* She shot a quick look over toward Pres. He was watching with a concerned look on his face.

"Why don't you go get a girl a drink? I've got a lot of catching up to do. I'll meet you . . . outside by the back benches," Sam said. *I can't believe I'm doing this. I'm going to be in Japan soon. Why am I bothering with these people?* But somehow, Sam couldn't stop herself.

"Sure thing, sweetheart," Taylor said to her solicitously. "You just wait right outside." He went speedily to the bar.

Sam went outside all right, but when Taylor came back to meet her, she wasn't there. She was in Mr. Jacobs's car, on the way back to the house.

She felt depressed, disgruntled, and frankly disgusted with her own behavior.

She hadn't even had a chance to talk with her friends or to tell Marina good-bye.

At least my birth certificate's coming, she thought. *Pretty soon I can get away from here—and start thinking about real life.*

NINE

Sam had never seen Becky so happy, but then again, she'd never, before that morning, heard Mr. Jacobs tell the twins that they could go clothes shopping courtesy of his American Express card. He'd even told Becky and Allie they shouldn't worry about how much money they spent. "Buy whatever you want, girls, you deserve it," Mr. Jacobs had said, handing over his card to Sam at the breakfast table.

"Dad, what are you feeling guilty about?" Becky had asked him.

"Not a thing," Mr. Jacobs said with an innocent grin. "Can't I just do something nice for my daughters?"

When Becky and Allie had gone upstairs to dress for the shopping expedition, Mr. Jacobs had taken Sam aside. "Sam, I'm hoping that maybe you can steer the twins toward some sort of middle ground, cloth-ingwise," he said with a sheepish look.

Aha! So that's his motive, Sam thought. *I'm supposed to do a double makeover.* "I can try," she said skeptically. What she wanted to add was that she'd try harder if she could add a few purchases of her own to his credit card, but she knew that would be pushing it.

"This hands-off parenting thing can get tough," he told Sam, almost as if he were apologizing to her.

Sam nodded sympathically. As far as she could see, Mr. Jacobs was doing a fairly crummy job of raising his daughters, but on the other hand, at least he was trying.

An hour later, Sam met Becky and Allie at the front door, ready to go. "We'll hit the Cheap Boutique," Sam said, naming the hippest place to shop on the island. "Your sergeant of shopping says that if you're gonna shop till you drop, you gotta buy early and often!"

As Sam maneuvered the car toward the Cheap Boutique, she thought about the fact that her birth certificate would finally arrive that day. The realization of what that meant sent a little shiver of anticipation through her. *The beginning of my new life,* she thought.

Loud rock music immediately assailed their ears as soon as Sam opened the door to the Cheap Boutique. If anything, it looked even wilder inside than it had last summer. New posters of various rock stars hung on the walls. A large-screen TV in the back showed music videos. Becky looked as if she had just landed in heaven. She made a beeline to the back of the store, where the spandex dresses and shorts were kept, while Allie hung around the entrance.

"Allie, aren't you going to come in?" Sam asked her.

"Sam, this is sinful," Allie said worriedly.

"What?" Sam asked.

"Sinful," Allie repeated.

"No, Allie," Sam responded. "Having someone else's credit card and *not* shopping—now *that* would be sinful," she joked.

Allie looked troubled. Sam could see she hadn't even appreciated the joke. *Okay, I'll try the reasonable approach,* Sam thought. "Look, Allie, it's not sinful until you buy something."

"You think so?" Allie asked.

"I know so," Sam said, nodding wisely. "So go inside and try on some stuff." Sam was astonished when her twisted logic worked and Allie actually went inside. *Well, hurray for me. I can still outsmart a fourteen-year-old*, she laughed to herself.

After browsing the racks for a while, Becky and Allie came out of the dressing rooms at the same time. They looked as different from each other as was humanly possible. Becky had put on a strapless black stretch minidress, black fishnet hose, and high-heeled red pumps, topping it off with a black beret. Allie wore an Indian peasant blouse, a long flowered cotton skirt, and hiking boots.

"I saw this relief worker on TV dressed like this," Allie said, looking in the mirror. "What do you think?"

Sam, wanting to be encouraging, said, "Why, Allie, I think you look just darling!"

"If you had a guitar, you'd be ready to sing some old hippie songs," Becky taunted her sister. "Do you know 'Puff the Magic Dragon'?"

As Becky and Allie glared at each other, Sam remembered that she was supposed to try to steer them both toward moderation. *Here goes nothing*, she thought.

"You know, Becky, I saw this cute girl in *Rock On* magazine wearing a dress like that," Sam said.

"Cool!" Becky breathed, admiring herself in a mirror.

"She had on plain panty hose and little black flats with it, though," Sam said. "It looked really hot."

"Really?" Becky said, obviously considering the idea.

"Well, it would certainly look better like that than it looks now," Allie said condescendingly. "You look like you could stand on a corner, peddling your—"

"Shows what you know!" Becky screamed, snatching the beret off her head. "Both of you! I'm buying this entire outfit," she said defiantly, disappearing into the changing area.

Sam turned to Allie. "What did you say that for?" she asked. "I just about had her convinced."

"She said something mean to me first," Allie mumbled, staring at the rug.

Great. Just great, Sam thought. *The two of them are regressing.*

Two hours later, Sam and the girls were ready to check out of the Cheap Boutique. Becky had purchased three other dresses in addition to the black one, and Allie had bought two shopping bags of clothes that she assured Sam she was going to give away to poor people.

"I see no reason why poor people shouldn't

be wearing nice new clothes instead of the rags that some rich person wants to give away," Allie said piously.

"Dad'll murderize you," Becky told her sister.

"The one he should murderize is you," Allie shot back hotly as they walked to the car. "Look at you—a spiritual cretin!"

"Do you see what I have to put up with?" Becky asked, rolling her eyes.

"You're both entitled to your own opinions," Sam said, starting the car.

"*I'm* entitled to my opinion," Becky said from the back seat. "Hers isn't an opinion because it's too loony."

"Becky!" Sam raised her voice. "Can you two take a breather, please?" She pulled the car into a parking space in front of the local five-and-dime. "I need to run in here for just a sec," Sam said. "Promise me you won't actually kill each other while I'm gone."

Sam went into the store, and came out a few minutes later carrying a small gift-wrapped package.

"What's that?" Becky asked. "For me?" She gave Sam her most ingratiating smile.

"Actually, it's for a friend of mine," Sam said, smiling back.

"Pres!" Becky said.

"He's so ho—I mean, he seems like a good person," Allie amended.

"I heard you! I heard you!" Becky hooted. "You were going to say how hot he is!"

"I wasn't, either," Allie mumbled, but her blush gave her away.

"Wrong, wrong, wrong," Sam told them as she pulled out of the parking space. "We're going to stop by the club on the way home so I can give this to Marina. It's her going-away present. She's leaving for Japan in a couple of days." *And I'm going with her in a few weeks!* she was dying to add, but she managed to keep her mouth shut.

Ten minutes later, they had negotiated the traffic of Main Street and made their way to the Sunset Country Club. Just as Sam had expected, her friend Marina was on her break.

Sam excused herself from the twins. Becky went to play video games in the game room, and Allie went into the club library.

Sam saw Marina sitting on a chaise lounge by the pool. She walked over to her friend, with the package behind her back.

"Well, if it isn't my compatriot in international crime," Marina said to her. "Next time we see each other, it'll be in Tokyo or Kyoto or Yokohama or something, sitting in a sushi bar drinking sake with the locals."

"I can't wait," Sam said, stretching out on a chair next to Marina's.

"Me neither," Marina said. "For the first time in my life, I'll be tall!"

Sam cracked up.

"I brought you something," Sam said a few moments later, a little sheepishly.

"What?" Marina asked, sitting up curiously.

"Oh, just something so you won't forget your friends on the island while you're dancing in Japan . . . and so you won't forget where you are," said Sam nonchalantly, thrusting her small present at Marina. She'd had it wrapped in paper decorated with cowboy hats.

Marina grinned and tore the package open. She laughed heartily as she plucked several tiny presents from it: a small Japanese flag, a small American flag, a tiny Japanese-English phrasebook, and a pair of porcelain earrings in the shape of Maine lobsters.

"This is fantastic," Marina said. "I don't get a lot of presents. I mean, growing up, it's mostly your parents who celebrate your birthday, and, well . . ." Marina let her voice trail off.

"Hey, we're *both* going to celebrate birthdays in Japan this year," Sam said, fingering the earrings she'd just given Marina. "We'll show them how two wild and crazy American girls have fun."

"Listen, I gotta get back in the high chair," Marina said, standing up and stretching. "I'm going back to New York tonight, and then my flight to Japan is the day after tomorrow."

"You'll be in exotic Japan, and I'll be in exotic Jacobs-land," Sam joked, getting up to leave.

"How 'bout I call you from there, tell you how it's going, get you psyched?" Marina asked.

"Great! A trans-Pacific phone call!" Sam exclaimed.

The two girls hugged. Then Marina went back to her last few hours of lifeguarding, while Sam went off in search of the twins.

A scant half-hour later, Sam and the twins walked in the door of the house, Sam's heart pounding wildly. *Oh my God oh my God oh my God it's here it's here it's here*, she thought. But she was wrong. There was no Package Express envelope waiting on the kitchen table, as she'd hoped. *Good grief— there was no one here to accept it! They probably tried to deliver it and since no one could take it they sent it back to Kansas.* Sam cursed her own stupidity.

Just then, a Package Express truck pulled into the driveway. *Yes!* Sam bounded out to meet the driver.

"Expecting something important, young lady?" the driver, a handsome uniformed black man in his thirties, asked with a smile.

"Sort of," Sam admitted.

"Is it from a sweetheart?" the driver asked.

"Nope," Sam said.

"A girl as pretty as you should be getting lots of presents," the man observed.

"Thank you," Sam said. What she was thinking was, *Please, do I have to deal with the Package Express man flirting with me? Just give me the darned envelope!* "Do you have an envelope from Kansas for Samantha Bridges?"

"Right here, miss. Just let me do a little paperwork . . . you sign right here . . . and here it is. Thank you for using Package Express, and have a nice day. I'll look forward to delivering anything else that you might have coming," the driver said with a flourish.

Hurray! My birth certificate! I can get my passport. Ladies and gentlemen, Samantha Bridges is outta here!

Sam grabbed the envelope and ran inside to the kitchen. The sun was shining, the birds were chirping, and yes, she finally had her birth certificate. Sam zipped open the envelope and reached inside.

STATE OF CALIFORNIA
OFFICIAL CERTIFICATE OF BIRTH

Mother: Susan Briarly   Father: Michael Blady

Address of mother:
1224 7th Avenue
San Francisco, California 94122

Address of father:
unknown

Name of child: SAMANTHA ELIZABETH BRIARLY
Sex: Female
Place of birth: Children's Hospital, San Francisco
Date of birth: May 24, 1973
Weight at birth: 7 pounds, 6 ounces

Attending physician: Dr. Ronald Cartwright
Childrens' Hospital
2376 Buena Vista Avenue
San Francisco, California 94113

Citizenship of mother: American
Citizenship of father: Israeli

TEN

Sam dropped the piece of paper on the kitchen table. This couldn't be happening. She sighed deeply and sat down hard in the nearest chair. There was a sick feeling in her stomach. *Maybe if I close my eyes,* Sam thought, *all of this will turn out to be a bad dream.* "How am I going to get a passport with this?" she said aloud. "The information's all wrong!" She squeezed her eyes shut as tightly as she could, but when she opened them again the strange names on the paper still sat there before her. *Mother: Susan Briarly. Father: Michael Blady. Name of child: Samantha Elizabeth Briarly.*

It obviously had to be some kind of mistake. Somehow her birth certificate had gotten mixed up with someone else's, or maybe some clerk somewhere had typed in the wrong information. Funny, though, that her parents had never noticed.

Mother: Susan Briarly. Father: Michael Blady. Name of child: Samantha Elizabeth Briarly. Sam shook her head.

"Hey, Sam, what's for lunch?" Becky asked, skidding into the kitchen. "I'm completely starved but I've got to lose . . ." Becky saw the look on Sam's face and moved closer to her. "Sam? Are you okay? What's wrong?"

"Nothing's wrong," Sam said in a flat voice. She had been so sure she'd be on her way to Japan soon, but now, because of some stupid mistake, she might lose her chance at starting her dream career. But she couldn't tell Becky any of this.

"Yes, there is," Becky said, sounding scared. She saw the white piece of paper on the table in front of Sam. "Does it have something to do with this?" Becky asked. She reached for the form, but Sam snatched it from her just in time.

"Leave me alone!" Sam cried, leaving her chair so abruptly that the chair fell over.

"Sam, come on, you're scaring me," Becky said.

"I've got to go make a phone call," Sam said, pushing past Becky.

144

Sam marched upstairs so she could use a phone in relative privacy. She dialed her parents' number directly, not caring for once how much the call would cost. Her mother answered on the first ring.

"Hello?"

"It's me," Sam said.

"Oh, Sam . . ." Her mother's voice trailed off.

"Listen, you guys were taking so long to send me my birth certificate that I asked Ruth Ann to do it, and I just got it. And somehow it's the wrong one! I can't believe you and Dad never noticed it!"

Sam could hear her mother breathing on the other end of the phone. The silence was deafening.

"Mom? Did you hear me?" Sam asked, beginning to panic. Something was wrong, she just knew it.

"Yes, honey, I heard you," her mother said. "It . . . it isn't the wrong one, Sam. I'm so very, very sorry that you're finding out this way," she continued, her voice choked.

"Finding out what?" Sam said, her voice rising with some terror she couldn't put a name to. "What are you telling me?"

"You . . . we adopted you, Sam," her mother said quietly.

The hallway started to spin around, and Sam had to lean against the wall to keep from falling.

"Sam? Are you there?" her mother asked. "Your father and I had planned to call to talk to you today, but Ruth Ann told me only ten minutes ago that she had sent you your birth certificate. . . ."

Sam gave a short, ugly laugh. "Is she adopted, too?"

"No, honey," her mother said. "After we adopted you we—"

"I don't want to hear about it!" Sam screamed. "How? How could you do this to me?"

"But Sam, we love you so!" her mother cried. "I know we should have told you sooner, but you have to understand that—"

"I don't have to understand *anything!*" Sam screamed, tears running down her face. "You lied to me! My whole life is a lie!"

"Oh, no, darling, that isn't true!" her mother said.

"When would you have told me if I hadn't asked for my birth certificate?" Sam sobbed. "Never?"

"We could never seem to find the right moment," her mother said lamely. "Please, Sam, your father and I want to talk with you—"

"My *father?*" Sam screamed. "Who the hell *is* my father?"

"Please, honey," Sam's mother begged, "let me call your dad at work and the three of us can—"

"You can what?" Sam interrupted. "Lie to me some more?"

"So we can explain, and try to—"

"I don't give a damn what you do!" Sam shouted into the phone. "I really don't. I hate you for this!" She slammed the phone down as hard as she could.

As soon as she did, though, she was sorry. With tears streaming down her face, she slid down the wall until she was sitting on the floor, sobbing. She felt as if she'd lost her parents. She felt as if she'd lost her life.

Becky and Allie came creeping up the stairs and stood there staring at her, their faces a ghostly white.

"What is it?" Allie whispered. "You can talk to us, really you can!"

"I have to get out of here," Sam mumbled to herself, using the wall to help get herself up.

"But where are you going?" Becky asked.

Sam didn't answer. She just ran down the stairs past the frightened twins.

With no destination in mind, Sam kept

running, as if somehow she could distance herself from the awful piece of paper that was burning a hole in her pocket. When she hit the beach she ran along the sand, as hard and as fast as she could. Faces were a blur as Sam pumped her legs painfully and dug her feet into the sand. She didn't stop running until she reached the far pier, and then she fell to her knees sobbing, her breath coming in gasps.

"Oh, please let this not be true!" Sam screamed into the air. But she knew it was. Her own mother had told her it was true. And all the screaming and wishing in the world wouldn't change a thing.

Sam sat there for what seemed like hours, staring out at the ocean, seeing nothing. When she started to shiver, she realized that the sun had gone behind some clouds and it looked like a storm was approaching.

I've got to talk to someone, Sam thought, *but who?* And then she knew. It had to be Carrie. Carrie was so sane, so smart, so truly kind and understanding—Sam would go see Carrie.

Although Graham and Claudia Templeton's house was about three miles away and up a hill, Sam didn't feel anything as she jogged the distance. She was on automatic pilot. The first splashes of rain hit her as she started up their hill, and the torrent began just as she reached their private driveway.

Sam knocked and Claudia opened the door.

"Sam! Are you okay?" she asked, taking in Sam's soaked clothes and wild-eyed appearance.

"I'm . . . I'm . . ." Sam stuttered.

"Well, get in out of the rain first!" Claudia said, holding the front door open wide.

"I'm dripping on your carpet," Sam said dully as a puddle formed around her.

"Forget about it," Claudia said. The worry was etched clearly on her face.

"Is Carrie here?" Sam asked, shivering.

"She's playing video games with the kids. I'll get her," Claudia said, "and she can find you some dry clothes."

In just a moment Carrie came bounding down the stairs, a worried expression in her eyes. It was obvious Claudia had told her how terrible Sam looked. Carrie touched her friend's arm. "Sam, what is it?" she asked softly.

Sam just stood there, shivering and unable to speak.

"Come on, let's go up to my room and I'll get you some dry clothes," Carrie said in a soothing voice. She led the practically coma-tose Sam up the stairs and helped her out of her wet clothes and into some sweats. Then she sat opposite her on the bed, calmly waiting for Sam to decide to speak.

"I got my birth certificate today," Sam began in a low voice.

"Right, for your passport. Your parents sent it," Carrie said, nodding.

"No, Ruth Ann did," Sam said. "She told me she saw it on my father's dresser, so I asked her to send it to me. I guess she never even looked at it. Or maybe she knew all along. . . ." she said, her voice choking up.

"Knew what?" Carrie asked.

Sam gulped hard. "Knew that I'm not her sister. Or my parents' daughter. Oh, Carrie . . . I'm adopted."

Carrie sat there for a moment, looking completely stunned. "Adopted?" she re-peated. "And they never told you?"

Sam shook her head. "I called my mom today. I figured it was some mistake. But she finally told me the truth," she said bitterly.

"What a terrible way for you to find out!" Carrie commiserated.

Sam looked at Carrie bleakly. "How could they do this to me? I just . . . I can't understand!"

Carrie sighed, visibly struggling to find words to comfort her friend. "They must really love you or they wouldn't have adopted you."

"How can I believe anything they say or do now?" Sam asked wildly. "If they'd lie to me about this, they'd lie about anything."

"Were they ever going to tell you the truth?" Carrie asked softly.

"How do I know?" Sam cried. "Whatever they tell me is bound to be another lie!" She got off Carrie's bed and paced around the room. "All my life I've felt different from them, acted different from them, looked different from them. All my life I've wondered why I don't fit in. Now I know why."

"Is Ruth Ann adopted, too?" Carrie asked.

"Oh, no, she's theirs," Sam said bitterly. "She looks just like my mother. My mother," Sam repeated. "I don't even know who my mother is."

"Oh, but you do!" Carrie said earnestly. "I mean, I know it sounds trite, but the person who raised you is your mother, don't you think?"

"Not if she could look me in the eye everyday for nineteen years and lie to me," Sam said softly.

"Do you know anything about . . . about what happened?" Carrie faltered.

Sam took her birth certificate out of the pocket of her rain-soaked pants and showed it to Carrie. "The joke's on me. All these years I envied girls from California, and it turns out I am one."

"I see your first name didn't change," Carrie said, attempting a small smile.

"That's the only thing that didn't," Sam answered. She sat down again next to Carrie. "Susan Briarly? Michael Blady? *Israel?* Who *are* these people?"

Carrie handed the birth certificate back to Sam. "I know how angry you feel," she said quietly, "but you need to call your parents and talk to them, give them a chance to explain."

"I hate them," Sam said in a dark voice.

"Oh, Sam, you don't mean that, you're just hurt."

"I *do* mean that," Sam repeated. "I never want to speak to them again as long as I live."

ELEVEN

Sam had one last thought before she finally drifted off into sleep: *Please, God, tell me I'm dreaming. Let this entire day be just one of the worst nightmares of my life. Let me wake up in a cold sweat. I'll take a long hot shower and this will all be behind me.*

But when Sam's eyes snapped open in the morning, she knew immediately it was no nightmare. *I'm adopted*, she thought. A wave of nausea swept over her. She hadn't eaten a thing, but even so she had to barf. She stumbled from her bed into the upstairs bathroom, bent over the toilet, and threw up.

All the time, a voice was sounding in her head. In a singsong, childish, teasing way, it said, *Samantha Bridges is adopted, Samantha Bridges is adopted!* Sam felt like she was going a little crazy, and she had no idea what to do about it.

She stumbled back to her bedroom, lay down on the bed, and put a cold washcloth over her eyes. She thought back to the day before, to exactly what had happened after she read the birth certificate that announced to the whole world what she had only just learned—that her mother and father were not her real mother and father.

It was a little scary, Sam admitted to herself, that she didn't remember much of the day before. She remembered reading the birth certificate. She remembered that her father—her biological father—was from Israel. *Israel?* She felt a twinge of soreness in her calf, and when she bent down to rub it she noticed that there were blisters on her feet. *That's right, I ran from here to the beach to Carrie's. That's miles!*

But she didn't recall how she had gotten back from the Templeton's house. Or how she'd gotten upstairs to her room. Or what she had said to Mr. Jacobs when he came home.

A rap on the door brought Sam back to the painful reality of the morning. Then there was another knock. Sam managed to croak out, "Who is it?"

"Sam?" asked Mr. Jacobs, a note of concern in his voice. "How do you feel this morning? The girls and I are really worried about you. Are you still sick?"

I must have told them that I had the flu or something, Sam thought. *What should I say now?* For one fleeting second she considered telling Mr. Jacobs the truth, because she wanted to tell someone, anyone, how bad she felt. Then she decided it was none of his damn business.

"Uh—I'm still feeling pretty lousy. I just threw up again," Sam said truthfully.

"Well," Mr. Jacobs said, "you take care of yourself, and I'll have Allie bring you some cereal."

Sam had no interest in either cereal or Allie. She was silent.

"Sam?" Mr. Jacobs asked solicitously. "Do you want some breakfast?"

"I think I want to sleep some more. I'll be down later," Sam answered in a weak voice.

"Okay. I'm sending the twins to the club on their own. I'll be there, too, playing golf. So if you need anything, just call the front desk, and they'll let one of us know."

"Okay, Mr. Jacobs." Sam heard the sound of his footfalls on the stairs and the bang of the screen door as he left with his kids for the club. Then the house was still.

What do I do now? Sam thought. Then she heard the screen door open and bang shut again.

"Sam?" Sam heard Carrie's voice calling out her name.

"Sam? It's us." Emma was with her.

Carrie and Emma climbed the stairs, opened the door to Sam's room, and found Sam stretched out on her bed, the washcloth still on her face.

Sam sat up and pulled her knees up tight to her chest, like a little kid.

Carrie and Emma sat down on the bed with Sam. It was Carrie who spoke first.

"Sam, I told Emma what happened. That's okay, right?"

Sam nodded.

"Sam, I'm not very good at this sort of thing," Emma said, blinking nervously. "But I just wanted to tell you from the bottom of my heart that you and Carrie have been the greatest friends I've ever had, and nothing in the world can change that. *Nothing*," she emphasized.

Sam nodded again.

"I just want you to know that I think I can imagine how hurt you feel," Emma continued, her gaze fixed on Sam. "My own mother and father have hurt me. I feel very bad that you feel bad," she said, this time brushing a few tears from her own cheek.

In a calm but quavery voice, Sam said, "You guys would never lie to me, I know that."

Carrie shifted her position a little before she responded. "Sam, this may sound really stupid now, but it means a lot to Emma and me that you can talk to us about what happened. I'm so happy to be your friend." Now Carrie was crying a little, too.

Sam fought back tears of her own and smiled a little. "Hey, if I can't dump my problems on you two, then who can I dump them on?" she asked.

"Can I get you a glass of juice, or something?" Emma asked.

Sam nodded gratefully. Then she stood up, walked over to the window, and looked out at the Jacobses' yard. *It looks the same as it did yesterday. Nothing's changed for anyone but me*, she thought.

Emma came back carrying a glass of orange juice. Sam rested it on the windowsill and then took a small sip as Emma and Carrie watched her from behind.

"What I can't stand," Sam said, talking out the window but addressing Carrie and Emma, "is that they lied to me! My own parents! And it's not like they were lying about what my great-grandfather did for a living, or whether my father ever failed a high school class."

Then Sam turned around to face her friends. "They lied about *me* to *me*," she said very slowly.

"How do you feel?" Carrie ventured.

"Incredibly pissed off and furious. Lost," Sam said bitterly, draining the rest of the juice and tossing the glass out the open window. They heard it shatter into a million pieces on the driveway. "Like that glass."

Carrie gasped involuntarily, and despite herself Sam smiled a little. *When she leaves she'll clean it up*, Sam thought. *That's Carrie, always cleaning up someone else's disaster*. Then Sam went back to feeling bad.

"Are you still planning to go to Japan?" Emma asked cautiously.

"Hell, yes. What do I need to stay here for? I can't think of a better time to go." Sam fairly spat out the words.

Carrie stood up, walked over to Sam's desk, and sat down in the oak chair. She picked up a pen and fiddled with it. "Sam, do you remember back when Graham fell off the wagon and started using drugs again?" Carrie asked.

"Sure. It was right after you shot those photos in Florida," Sam replied, moving back to the bed, where Emma still sat.

"Well, Claudia told me that after that, the whole family—Graham, Claudia, Ian, even Chloe—went to see this family therapist in New York City. She said it really helped," Carrie said thoughtfully.

"I'm not seeing any shrink in New York City," Sam shot back.

"Well, you wouldn't have to," Carrie said carefully. "This lady, Ms. Miller, spends part of her summer right here on Sunset Island. I'm sure that she would talk to you." She handed Sam a piece of paper with a name and phone number on it. "I got this from Claudia," Carrie said. "I didn't say it was for you or anything," she added hastily.

"I don't need what's-her-name," Sam said bitterly, crumpling the paper up and sticking it in the pocket of the sweatshirt she had on. "I need a new life."

Mr. Jacobs and the twins came home from the club in the early afternoon. They found Sam sitting at the kitchen table with an unread magazine open before her.

"Hey, glad to see you're feeling better!" Mr. Jacobs exclaimed, not even noticing that he was tracking mud across the floor.

159

"Dad! Look at the floor!" Becky exclaimed. "You'd kill me if I did that!"

Sam felt like she was watching this scene in a movie. *He said he was glad I'm feeling better, but he has no clue how I really feel. And the twins—doesn't he realize that he pays no real attention to them?*

Sam suddenly felt she had to get out of there. "I'm going for a walk on the beach," she announced in a quiet voice. "I think the ocean air would be good for me. Anyone want to come?" But the steel in her voice made it clear she wasn't interested in company. No one answered, and she left alone.

At the beach, she took her usual walk to the far pier and back. It was a glorious summer day, and the main beach was filled with people, blaring radios, kids throwing Frisbees and footballs, even a game of volleyball. But to Sam it all seemed very far away. *Like a movie*, she thought. *Am I really part of this?*

Sam heard someone call out her name as she walked by. She saw Diana De Witt and Lorell Courtland stretched out on two straw mats on the sand, their perfect bodies glistening under the sun.

"Well, if it isn't *the* Samantha Bridges, famous X-rated model!" Diana called out to her.

Sam just kept walking, not even casting a glance in their direction. Sam usually never backed down from an insult, but this time she wasn't taking the bait.

When she got to the pier, Sam stopped and looked out at the ocean. *It's the same ocean as yesterday*, she thought. *The same waves. So why do I feel like I'm on a different planet?*

She walked all the way back to the Jacobses' house without stopping. There was a scrawled message from Mr. Jacobs on her bed: *Sam—Your parents called from the Sunset Inn. Is everything okay? I didn't know you were expecting them. They want you to call ASAP.*

My parents. On the island. Something painful tugged at Sam's heart, but she forced the feeling away and clenched her hands into fists. *I'll call them when I damn well please. And I'll see them when I damn well please, too. Who do they think they are, Batman and Robin coming to save the day?*

The phone rang again. Sam answered it without thinking. "Jacobs residence," she said dully.

"Sam, it's us," a familiar voice said.

It was her mother.

Twenty minutes later her mother and

father came by in a rental car, picked up Sam, and drove her back to the Sunset Inn. It was a silent ride. Her parents tried to get her to talk to them about how she felt, but all Sam would repeat was: "I have nothing to say to you."

They went out to the rear veranda of the Sunset Inn, which was deserted except for a couple of seagulls sitting at the top of the wooden stairway leading down to the ocean. Mr. and Mrs. Bridges sat down on rocking chairs. Sam stood.

"Sam, I wish you would sit and talk with us," Mrs. Bridges said gently.

No answer. Then Sam said, with measured words, "And if I do, what do I call you? *Mom and Dad?*"

Sam's father rocked gently. "I know you must want to hear how we came to adopt you. Please sit down, and I'll tell you. Because when you know why we brought you into our family, and why we didn't tell you all these years, maybe you won't be so angry with Carla and me."

Carla. He called Mom Carla. Sam sat down.

In even tones, her father told Sam the story of how, after he and his wife had tried for a year to conceive a child, they had gone to a doctor in Topeka.

"The doctor told us that the problem was with me, not with your mother," he said.

"But we wanted a child so badly!" her mother added passionately. "We had so much love to give. So we went to an adoption agency, and a year later, we went out to San Francisco to pick you up."

Yeah, great, Sam said to herself. *As if I were a container of mushrooms in the produce section of the supermarket.* Her face remained stony.

"Then about eighteen months later, I conceived Ruth Ann," her mother continued. "It was totally unexpected. The doctor said it just happens that way sometimes."

Sam looked from her mother to her father, and then back at her mother. She gripped the arms of the rocking chair tightly.

"But why didn't you tell me?" Sam shouted. "How am I supposed to feel now? Like you get on the airplane to come to talk to me three weeks before I go to Japan and everything's okey-dokey?"

Mr. and Mrs. Bridges sat in silence.

"And what if I hadn't gotten the job? You would never have told me?" Sam yelled, so loudly that the seagulls became frightened and flew away.

"We would have told you," Mr. Bridges said quietly.

"Yeah, right," Sam retorted. "When I was looking through the safe-deposit box after you both died."

Her parents sat looking stunned and guilty and sad. They both stared at the ground.

"Sam, the first thing you must know is that your father and I love you as much as we could love anything or anyone," her mother began in a shaky voice. "We love *both* our daughters as much as we could love anything or anyone."

Sam rocked and looked down at the wooden deck.

"We did a stupid thing, Sam," she continued. "Lord, did we do a stupid thing. I guess you and your friends must think parents are professionals at doing stupid things."

Sam didn't look up. The boards of the deck were a blur through her tears.

"We meant to tell you. We really did. But every time we were going to, we were afraid it would hurt you," her mother said, as gently as she could. "Or it wasn't the right time. Or *we* weren't ready. Or we convinced ourselves you didn't need to know. So we didn't say anything. But it's not too late to talk now."

"Yes, it is," Sam said. "There's such a

thing as too little, too late. And this is *way* too little, *way* too late. I think I should go now."

Sam left.

TWELVE

Sam stood underneath the hot water and let it cascade over her face and body. She turned the tap all the way, but not even the scalding water could penetrate the horrible, dead feeling that surrounded her.

"Sam? Are you up?" came the voice of one of the twins, calling from her doorway.

Sam turned off the water and wrapped herself in a towel, then walked into her room.

A concerned-looking Allie stood in the doorway. "Are you okay?" she asked uncertainly.

"I'm okay," Sam said, her voice expressionless.

"Pres called for you just now," Allie said. "I told him you'd call him back."

Sam didn't answer. She just went back into the bathroom to get her robe from the hook on the back of the door. Funny how unimportant Pres seemed now. Who cared if Diana flirted with him, or if he flirted back? What difference could it possibly make?

"So . . . are you over the flu?" Allie asked, biting her lower lip.

"I guess," Sam answered in a hollow voice. "I'll get dressed and be right down."

Sam threw on some cutoff jeans and the same sweatshirt she had worn the day before, paying absolutely no attention to how she looked. She pulled her hair back in a ponytail and left her face free of makeup.

When she got downstairs, Becky and Allie both stared at her with alarm.

"Wow, you really do look sick," Becky said as she popped her toast out of the toaster. "Want me to make you some breakfast or something?"

Sam almost smiled at that. *Imagine Becky offering to make breakfast for me.* "I'll just have some coffee," she said.

"Dad went to the market to get you some of that great fresh-squeezed orange juice," Allie said. "He thought it might make you feel better."

Becky sat opposite Sam as she sipped her coffee in silence. "If there was something, like, seriously wrong with you, you'd tell us, wouldn't you?" she asked.

"What she means is, you wouldn't have some horrible illness and then just leave us one day and not tell us, would you?" Allie clarified.

Sam felt guilt wash over her. Maybe she should have told the twins she was leaving for Japan in just a few weeks. She couldn't very well let them think she had some horrible illness. "I'm not sick, not that kind of sick," Sam said, stirring her coffee slowly.

"What kind of sick, then?" Allie asked, sitting down next to her sister.

Sam looked from one face to the other. "I really can't talk about it," she told them.

Allie bit her lower lip and studied the tabletop intently. "It's just that . . . well, our mom, she used to say she had headaches all the time. And then one day she was just gone."

"We thought it was us," Becky explained. "We were only six. Dad just kept saying Mom wasn't feeling well, and that we should leave her alone. And one day we came home early from this weekend ski trip with Dad," Allie continued in a low voice. "because Becky had a stomachache . . ."

"I remember I was standing there in the hall," Becky said, staring out into the distance, "and I wanted Mom to make my stomach feel better. And then we heard these sounds from Mom and Dad's bedroom, a man and a woman laughing, and the woman was Mom . . ."

"Dad made us go next door to the Clintons' house," Allie finished. "And we never saw Mom again."

"Not ever?" Sam asked, truly horrified by their story.

"Nope," Becky said. "Aunt Natalie says Mom ran off with this real young guy, but Dad won't talk about it."

"Aunt Natalie says Mom just had to 'look for her own life.'" Allie added. "Sometimes I wonder if we'll ever see her again. And if it was our fault."

"It wasn't your fault," Sam assured her.

Allie just shrugged. "Anyway, you've been acting so weird that we just wondered . . ."

"It's nothing like that," Sam said quietly. She looked at their anxious faces and decided to level with them. After all, they had just told her a very personal and painful story about their own lives. "The truth is," Sam began, taking a deep breath, "I just found out that I'm adopted."

For a long moment there was total silence in the room.

"Adopted?" Becky repeated, her eyes as bit as saucers. "You mean you never knew before?"

"Bingo," Sam said bitterly. "And I only found out by accident. My parents flew in to try to 'explain' it to me. That's where I went last night—to see them at the Sunset Inn."

Allie looked at Becky. "Wow, can you imagine finding out something like that?"

Becky shook her head. "I would hate it."

"Well, at least I know you really are my sister—no hiding that," Allie said.

"Oh yeah? Well, then, why do you try so hard?" Becky asked, her chin jutting out angrily.

"I just don't want to be like Mom, okay?" Allie said defensively. "I don't want to be some weird person who runs off with guys. . . ." Allie's voice trailed off.

Oh God, Sam thought, *that's what's scaring her so much.* "Listen, Allie," she began gently, "you can like guys and dress nicely and not turn into a . . . a person with problems."

Allie looked skeptical. "Becky acts just like how I figure Mom did—"

"I do not!" Becky cried.

"Neither one of you has to be like her," Sam said. "Each of you is completely her own person."

Becky looked at Sam and cocked her head to one side. "I guess you don't even know what you could inherit," she said thoughtfully.

Sam felt a lump in her throat. "No, I don't."

"Fresh-squeezed juice!" Mr. Jacobs sang out as he walked in the front door with a bag of groceries. "I've got carrot, orange, and grapefruit." Then he saw the serious look on Becky, Allie, and Sam's faces and stopped talking. "I guess you told them about Japan, huh?" he said after a moment. "That's why all the long faces."

"What?" Allie asked, but her father didn't hear her.

"I was going to tell you, girls, I just couldn't find the right moment. I knew you would be really upset."

Sam slammed her coffee cup down more loudly than she had intended. "What is it with parents? Why do you go around keeping important things from your kids?" Sam knew she was thinking more about her own parents than she was about Mr. Jacobs, but he was guilty, too.

"Dad, what are you talking about?" Becky demanded.

Mr. Jacobs put down the bag of juice.

"You didn't tell them? Well, I just messed that up totally, didn't I?"

Sam pushed herself out of her chair and stood up. "If you don't mind, I'll go for a walk and let you discuss this as a family." The word *family* had an ironic ring to Sam's ears.

"Thanks, Sam," Mr. Jacobs said. "I think I'll take the girls out on the water for the afternoon so we can talk."

"Which one of your bimbos is coming with us?" Becky asked.

"It'll be just us," her father said, smiling sheepishly at Sam.

At least I'm out of here, Sam thought, grabbing her rhinestone-studded baseball cap and her purse from the desk in the hall on her way out the door.

Sam headed for the beach without any specific destination in mind. It was so hard to plan, to think of what to do. One part of her wanted to run over to the Sunset Inn to see her parents, and another part of her never wanted to see them again. She felt torn apart inside, crazy, and empty, all at the same time. *I don't know how to deal with this!* Sam thought desperately. *I don't know what I should do.* She ducked her head so that passersby would not see the tears that sprang to her eyes, and she thrust her hands in the pockets of her sweatshirt.

Her fingers curled around a slip of paper, and she pulled it out of her pocket. *Irma Miller*, the paper read in Carrie's neat handwriting. There was a phone number.

Was this what she should do, talk with some stranger about her life? What if it was horrible and embarrassing? What if this therapist hated her?

And then without having any answers, Sam found herself crossing the boardwalk to the nearest pay phone. She dropped in a quarter and dialed the number on the paper.

"Hello?" came a pleasant female voice.

Sam's heart beat a tattoo in her chest. "Uh, is this Irma Miller?"

"Yes, it is," the voice answered patiently. "And this is . . . ?"

"Samantha Bridges," Sam answered, trying to keep her voice from shaking. "I'm a friend of Carrie Alden—she works for Claudia and Graham Templeton."

"Yes?" the voice encouraged calmly.

"Well . . . Carrie gave me your number," Sam rushed on. "I hope it's okay to call you, I know you're on vacation and everything . . ."

"Actually, I'm seeing a few clients here

174

this summer," Ms. Miller said. "And it's fine that you called. Is something on your mind?"

"Yes, well, the thing is, I . . . I just found out that I'm adopted. I'm nineteen, so I guess it shouldn't matter, so I guess I'm just bothering you. . . ." Sam had to stop talking because she was sobbing so hard. "I'm . . . I'm really sorry," she managed to gasp.

"It's okay," Ms. Miller said. "That must be a great shock to you."

"Yes, yes, it is!" Sam cried. "I don't know what to do!"

"Would you like to come over and talk with me?" Ms. Miller suggested. "Perhaps that would help."

"Could I?" Sam asked. She felt as if someone was throwing her a lifeline.

"Sure, it's fine," Ms. Miller said. "I'm in the big green house at the end of Ocean Drive, on the bay side. Know it?"

"I can find it," Sam said. "Is it okay if I come right now?"

"It is," Ms. Miller confirmed.

Sam walked the short distance to Irma Miller's house and nervously knocked on the front door of the green-shuttered clapboard house. A slender, attractive woman in her fifties answered the door.

"Hi, you must be Samantha," the woman said, holding out her hand. "I'm Irma Miller."

"You can call me Sam," Sam said in a small voice that she hardly recognized as her own.

They walked back into a cozy-looking room filled with plants. A green and white print sofa sat opposite a leather chair. Sam sat gingerly on the sofa, and Ms. Miller sat in the chair.

"So," Ms. Miller began, "you sounded very distressed on the phone."

Sam nodded.

"Do you want to tell me about it?"

Sam took a deep breath and began the story from the point where she'd called to tell her parents about her job offer to dance in Japan. She didn't stop talking until she had described her conversation with them the night before.

"They say they love me," Sam concluded bitterly. "That's a joke. You don't treat someone you love like that."

Ms. Miller nodded thoughtfully. "Have you always gotten along well with your parents in the past?"

Sam shrugged. "Okay, I guess. I mean, I always felt different. I never did fit in."

"Really?" Ms. Miller said, nodding with interest.

"I'm nothing like them, or like my sister, Ruth Ann, either. They all love living in this gruesome little town in Kansas. I always hated it. I've always had these dreams, you know? Of going somewhere else and doing something great."

"So you weren't very happy in Kansas?" Ms. Miller prompted.

Sam gave a snort. "To say the least. I remember once asking my mother how I'd wound up in this family. I said it like a joke, you know, because I'm so different from them."

"And what did she say?" Ms. Miller asked.

Sam looked at the floor. "She kissed the top of my head and said how much she loved me."

"Do you think maybe she wanted to tell you then, but she didn't know how?"

Sam gave the therapist a steely-eyed look. "It was her job—hers and my father's. It was their obligation to tell me."

"But now that you know, and you look back," Ms. Miller said, "do you think there were moments when your parents may have wanted to tell you, but they couldn't find the right way to do it?"

Sam stared out the window at a little girl

jumping rope. "I always felt—I don't know—something. Like there was some mystery, something I didn't know . . ."

"So on one level you kind of suspected something," Ms. Miller said slowly.

"It's so weird," Sam whispered, continuing to look out the window at the little girl. "One minute everything in your life makes sense, and then—*boom*—nothing does."

"Your parents really hurt you," Ms. Miller said softly.

Sam nodded, and tears fell silently down her cheeks. "Now the world seems too scary. I always felt that, no matter what, Mom and and Dad would be there for me. But I was wrong. They totally betrayed me. I don't know who they are at all, and I sure as hell don't know who I am."

Ms. Miller nodded thoughtfully. "You said your parents are here on the island?"

Sam nodded. "I talked to them last night. It was horrible."

"What would you think about having them come in with you tomorrow, and the four of us could talk?"

"I have nothing to say to them," Sam said in a flat, angry voice.

"You could listen, then," the therapist suggested. "It might make you feel better."

"I doubt it," Sam said bluntly.

"Think about it," Ms. Miller urged, standing up, "and call me later to let me know. Will you do that?"

Sam stood up and wiped the last of her tears from her eyes. "I'll think about it."

That was as much of a promise as she could make.

THIRTEEN

The next morning, Becky and Allie sat at the foot of Sam's bed as she stood in front of the mirror brushing her hair. Sam was on her way to Irma Miller's, where she had made arrangements to meet her parents. And even though she was as nervous and upset as she'd ever been in her life, she couldn't help noticing that Becky and Allie were both dressed in plain old jeans and sweatshirts. Sam didn't want to risk commenting on this miracle, lest one of them take it as some sort of challenge.

"So, did this lady act like she was on your side?" Allie asked, digging her toes into Sam's comforter.

"Not on my side, exactly," Sam said, fishing her mascara out of the bottom of her purse. "But not *not* on my side, either."

"I'm glad to see you're putting on some

makeup," Becky commented as she watched Sam. "No offense, but you don't look so fabulous without it. Your eyelashes are so pale."

Sam stopped brushing the mascara onto her lashes and stared at herself in the mirror. Her eyelashes *were* pale without mascara. Where had she gotten that from? Was her birth mother a redhead, too? That horrible feeling that had been with Sam ever since she learned the truth clutched at her stomach again. That stupid singsong voice once again assaulted her mind: *Sam is adopted, Sam is adopted!*

The phone rang in the hall and Becky ran to get it.

Sam looked at Allie. "No contest to get the phone?"

Allie shrugged and looked thoughtful. Obviously something else was on her mind. "I guess it's true, about you leaving for Japan in a few weeks."

Sam nodded. "I wasn't trying to hide it from you," she said. "I just thought your dad should be the one to tell you."

Becky came back into the room with a disgusted look on her face. "Some guy said he was taking a survey. Then he asked me what color nightie I slept in."

"I hope you hung up," Sam said.

"No, I invited him over," Becky snorted. "Of course I hung up."

The phone rang again. "Maybe it's the perv!" Becky sang out, and ran to get the phone again.

"I guess it hasn't been very much fun being here with us lately," Allie said, not looking at Sam.

What do I tell her—that's she's right? Sam wondered. She sat down on the bed next to Allie. "Sometimes it is tough with the two of you," she admitted. "But that doesn't mean I don't like you, or that I don't like my job here, because I really do."

"Really?" Allie asked doubtfully.

"Really," Sam confirmed, and she found she meant it with all her heart.

Allie sighed. "I guess I understand. You want to go off and have adventures."

"And a career," Sam added.

"Yeah, that," Allie agreed. "It just won't be the same with some dumb stranger here."

To Sam's surprise, she saw tears in the corners of Allie's eyes. *It must be so hard to have your mother abandon you, and then have that feeling stay with you your whole life,* Sam thought. Then she realized some-

183

thing. *Oh, God, my mother abandoned me, too*, she thought, her guts wrenching again.

Sam rose briskly from the bed and turned away from Allie. "Look, I don't really have time to talk about this now," she said. In her head she added, *Can't you see I've got my own problems to worry about?*

"Hey, Sam, the phone's for you," Becky said from the doorway.

"Don't tell me," Sam said. "He wants to know if I sleep in the nude."

Becky laughed. "I don't know. It's Pres. Want me to go ask him for you?"

Sam shooed her away and went to pick up the phone.

"Hey there," Pres drawled when Sam had said hello. "Becky was just tellin' me how much she loves motorcycles. I had to promise to take her for a ride one day."

"Uh-huh," was all Sam said.

"Uh-huh?" Pres repeated incredulously. "No smart comeback? No warning me that I'd be takin' my life in my hands?"

"Do whatever you want," Sam said hollowly.

There was silence on the other end of the phone.

"Sam? What's wrong?" Pres finally asked, his voice full of concern.

"Nothing," Sam answered. She wasn't about to confide in Pres. Her relationship with him was teasing, flirtatious, fun. No way was she going to go to him with her problems.

"Hey, sweetheart, it sounds like something," Pres said softly. "Maybe I can help."

The image of Pres grinning appreciatively at Diana De Witt flashed into Sam's brain. *Right*, she thought. *He's the last person I'm going to talk to.* "Listen, I'm kind of busy now," she said into the mouthpiece. "Maybe we could talk later."

"Anytime, Sam," Pres said quietly.

"Yeah, well, bye," Sam said, hanging up. For a moment there she had thought she might actually tell him everything. But no, that would be stupid. First of all, she didn't have that kind of a relationship with him. And second of all, she couldn't stand girls who acted all sappy and went running to guys to make everything okay.

Sam looked at her watch. She had only fifteen minutes to get over to Irma Miller's house. Part of her just wanted to run away. But she forced herself to walk calmly into her bedroom to get her purse and the car keys.

"So, I hope it goes okay and everything," Becky said.

"Me, too," Allie added.

"Thanks," Sam said, managing a smile. Just when she thought these girls were the most impossible duo in history, they said or did something endearing. "Hey, if you mess up the bed, make it again, okay?" Sam added on the way out.

"You never make it, why should we?" Becky yelled at Sam's retreating form.

On second thought, they're the same old monsters, Sam decided, running down the stairs.

As Sam drove toward the therapist's house she thought about the brief conversation she'd had with her parents the day before. After leaving Ms. Miller's house, she'd walked around for hours, her mind a blank. She had wanted to call her parents, and then again, she hadn't. But finally something had made her go dial the Sunset Inn—maybe the same something that had made her call the therapist.

Her parents had been so grateful for Sam's call that for a moment she'd felt guilty about how she was treating them. But a split second later all her anger came back. She was completely in the right. They had betrayed her, and she could never trust them again.

Briefly, she'd asked her parents if they wanted to go talk with the therapist. They'd agreed immediately. "I don't think it will do any good," Sam had told them before she hung up.

Well, I feel exactly the same way I felt yesterday, Sam told herself as she pulled into Ms. Miller's driveway. Just then the car her parents had rented pulled in right behind her. How bizarre it felt, looking at those two familiar faces and seeing strangers. The threesome awkwardly walked up to the front door and rang the bell.

When they had all settled down in Ms. Miller's pleasant office, the therapist asked Sam to relate once again how she saw the events that had unfolded.

"And that's it," Sam said when she'd finished. "That's the whole story."

"Well, it's never the whole story, really," Ms. Miller said with a kind smile. "That started a long time before you found out you were adopted."

"Well, sure," Sam agreed irritably. "Way back when they decided to bring this lovely bundle of joy into their home. And then there was every single year of my life that they lied to me. We could start way back there."

Sam's parents stared at the rug. It seemed they couldn't even face her.

"I'd like to start even before that," the therapist suggested. "Mrs. Bridges, what was your family like?"

Sam's mother seemed surprised at the question. "Well, they're lovely people. I grew up on a farm, with all kinds of pets."

"And your parents?" Ms. Miller prompted.

"Strict, I suppose you could say," Mrs. Bridges said. "They loved all us kids, but we were supposed to be seen and not heard."

The therapist nodded thoughtfully. "And you, Mr. Bridges?" she asked.

"My father died when I was ten," Sam's father said in a quiet voice. "And my mother was—and is—something of a character. She was a women's libber way before her time. People considered her a nut. I was terribly embarrassed by her when I was a kid," he added.

"She's the only one in the family I can relate to at all," Sam put in.

"So what I'm hearing," Ms. Miller began, "is that you, Mrs. Bridges, grew up in a family where parents didn't really talk with their children."

"That's true," Sam's mother agreed.

"And you, Mr. Bridges, spent a good portion of your youth in a single-parent household where you felt alienated from your mother."

Mr. Bridges nodded.

"We're all a product of the families we come from," the therapist explained. She looked at Sam. "Can you see that your parents, coming from the backgrounds they do, might have a difficult time telling you about your adoption?"

"No," Sam said bluntly.

"No?" Ms. Miller repeated.

"Okay, difficult, maybe," Sam allowed. "But that's just too bad. I mean, it was their responsibility. They were just too selfish to tell me."

"Oh, that's not true!" Sam's mother cried.

"We wanted to tell you, so many times," her father explained.

"Yeah, you told me all this the other night," Sam said with disgust. She looked at the therapist. "I told you this was a waste of time."

"There's no instant fix here," Ms. Miller acknowledged. "Sam feels very hurt—rightly so—and this is going to take some time and some work. She feels very angry that you never told her the truth about how she came

189

into your family," the therapist told Sam's parents.

"Yes, we know," Sam's father answered. "If we could only undo it . . ."

"But you can't," Sam said bluntly.

"No, you can't," Ms. Miller agreed. "But you can come to some new understanding about what happened, and you can learn to move forward." The therapist leaned toward Sam. "Sam, can you acknowledge that your parents had a difficult time telling you?"

"Maybe," Sam muttered.

"And can you think of times they tried to tell you, but then couldn't follow through? Times that perhaps you suspected something, but didn't want to know?"

"Maybe," Sam said again. "But that doesn't make it my fault!"

"That's right, it's not your fault," the therapist agreed. "But it might help you to understand what was going on with your parents."

"I'd like to say something," Sam's father said, clearing his throat.

Sam noticed that the hair at his temples was turning gray, and the lines around his eyes seemed pronounced. *My daddy*, Sam thought. *No, he isn't my daddy.*

"When Sam was a child, we read all these books on how to tell your child she's adopted," Sam's dad began earnestly. "They all said we should tell our daughter that she was extra special because we had chosen *her* to love."

"But that bothered us," Sam's mother continued, "because when Sam was two, I gave birth to Ruth Ann. It seemed to us that if we told Samantha that, it was like saying Ruth Ann wasn't as special. We didn't want Ruth Ann to feel bad, either."

Ms. Miller nodded. "Yes, I can understand that. Can you, Sam?"

Sam shrugged. She didn't see how this really changed anything.

"And then there was this family we knew from church," Sam's mom said. "Ever since their little adopted boy was old enough to understand, they told him how special he was. Well, this little boy was a wreck. He was nervous and anxious all the time. It seemed like he felt some kind of . . . pressure . . ."

"Right!" Sam's father agreed. "That boy thought he had to live up to this title of being 'special' all the time. We didn't want to do that to our daughter."

Ms. Miller nodded thoughtfully. "I've heard this from other adoptive parents before," she said. "I think it's very difficult to know the best way to handle this—"

"But that doesn't mean you don't handle it at all!" Sam interjected.

"True," the therapist agreed. "Let's talk about what your parents could have said that might have worked for you."

"What difference does it make now?" Sam yelled. She got up from her chair. "This is a total waste of time!"

"Please, Sam, sit down. I know you're angry, but leaving will only make you feel worse."

Sam sat down and folded her arms. "Fine," she snapped.

"It seems to me," the therapist began slowly, "that there are different ways of coming into a family, all equally valid. You can be born into a family, you can marry into a family, you can be adopted into a family. And no way is better than any other way."

Sam's mother nodded eagerly and looked at Sam. "Family is family," she said, a pleading look on her face.

"I wish we had thought of it that way years ago," Sam's father said with a sigh. "It makes perfect sense to me."

Sam looked at him. "Are you saying that if you'd thought of explaining it the way Ms.

Miller just did, you'd have told me the truth?"

Her father smiled a sad smile. "Honestly, Sam, I just don't know. I'd like to think so."

"Me, too," her mother added quietly. "You've been our daughter since you were a little baby. We've never thought of you as anything else."

"I have no reason to believe you," Sam said, staring at the carpet.

"Have your parents generally told you the truth in the past?" the therapist asked.

"Who knows anymore?" Sam asked.

"I think you know," Ms. Miller said. "Have they?"

"Yes," Sam mumbled honestly.

"So why does one sin of omission— admittedly a big one, but it's still only one— why does that cancel out all the honesty and love you've shared as a family for your whole life?"

"Maybe it shouldn't," Sam whispered, "but it's how I feel."

"Well, this new circumstance in your life is going to take time to adjust to," Ms. Miller told them. "And it's going to require a lot more communication among the three of you."

"We don't get to see Sam much these days," Mr. Bridges said sadly.

"Well, that's something the three of you can discuss," Ms. Miller said, rising from her chair. "And I do hope you *will* keep discussing this. I would urge you to bring Ruth Ann in on it, too." She walked them to her front door. "Good luck," she said with a warm smile, "and if there's anything else I can do, please call me."

Sam and her parents walked silently to their cars.

"I wish I had thought about telling you that there were simply different ways of becoming family," Sam's mother said. "It somehow makes things sound so easy."

"I wish you had, too," Sam answered.

"We have a flight back to Kansas tonight," Mrs. Bridges said. "Dad has to get back to work. I wish we could stay. . . ."

"It's okay," Sam said dully.

"I guess you're still planning to take this job in Japan," her father said.

"I guess," Sam replied.

"We wish you wouldn't," her mother said timidly. "It's just that we have so much talking to do now, and you'd be so far away. . . ."

"I need some time to think," Sam said. "I just don't feel sure of anything right now."

"Well, you can be sure of one thing," her

father said, sadness and determination etched on his face. "We love you. No matter how mad you are at us, or even if you decide never to speak to us again, we love you. Nothing can change that. Ever."

Sam's eyes blurred with tears as she got into Mr. Jacobs's car. When she pulled out of the driveway, she turned in one direction and her parents turned in the other. She didn't know when she'd see them, or even speak with them, again.

But she knew it was completely up to her.

FOURTEEN

When Sam pulled into the driveway at the Jacobses' house, the sight of a familiar-looking motorcycle with a gorgeous, lanky guy leaning against it greeted her.

"Waiting long?" Sam asked as she stepped out of the car.

"Not very," Pres said. "Anyway, I was entertained by the twins. They were tryin' to convince me that the Flirts should write a song about them."

"Did it work?" Sam asked.

"You cut me to the quick, girl," Pres said, slapping his hand over his heart. "The Flirts have to be truly *inspired* to write a song about someone. Now, I could write a song about you, maybe," he added, a teasing look on his face.

"Thanks for the offer," Sam said politely.

"Listen, it was nice of you to stop by, but I should go in and check on the girls."

"Lucky you. They went to play golf with their daddy," Pres drawled.

"Mr. Jacobs got the twins to go play *golf?*" Sam asked incredulously.

Pres shrugged. "Allie said somethin' about twin seventeen-year-olds working as caddies who both look like Luke Perry."

"Allie said that? Don't you mean Becky?" Sam asked.

"Nope, the one with the short hair," Pres answered. "That girl had one lovestruck look on her face."

"Well, will wonders never cease," Sam marveled. "I guess this means she isn't going to become a nun."

"Not today," Pres agreed with a grin. "So how about we go for a ride?"

Suddenly the thought of riding behind Pres on his bike sounded really appealing. "You're on," Sam said, accepting the helmet Pres handed her.

As Pres drove the wind rushed at Sam's face and whipped her hair into her eyes. She inhaled the salty air deeply as they got closer to the ocean. For the first time in days she felt a little better.

Pres parked, and he and Sam wandered

along the sand for a while. "This is just about my favorite place on this whole island," Pres said, flopping down on the beach.

Sam sat next to him quietly for a moment. They were in an area of tall dunes on the bay side of the island. Kurt Ackerman had brought them all there the summer before, because it was one of his favorite places, too. Quiet, isolated, private—it was hard to believe that wealthy vacationers abounded just on the other side of those dunes. But here in this private place, their thoughts were disturbed by nothing more than a calling gull.

"You sounded real upset on the phone, Sam," Pres said after a while.

Sam lifted a handful of sand and sifted it through her fingers. "I know I was rude. I'm sorry."

"Well, as we say back home, that don't make no never mind," Pres drawled. "I wasn't looking for an apology."

"Well, you got one anyway," Sam said.

Pres was quiet for a moment, staring into the blue sky. "There's something about you that always wants to keep me at arm's length," he said slowly. "It's hard to know who you really are."

"What is this, Psychology 101?" Sam asked.

"See, that's just what I mean," Pres said seriously. "I want to be your friend, and real friends talk to each other."

Sam shot Pres a look. "And here I always thought that 'I want to be your friend' meant 'You're not cute enough to be my girlfriend.'"

Pres grinned. "Well, you *must* know better than that. But seriously, how can we even talk about this girlfriend-boyfriend stuff when we can't even get past friend, period?"

Sam stared at him. "Yo, time out, bucko. Last summer you wanted me to go away with you overnight and stay in the same room—I don't imagine we were going to discuss philosophy all night. So what is this line you're handing me?"

Pres scratched his chin thoughtfully. "Ever think that maybe people change?"

"Meaning you no longer want to get into my pants?" Sam asked, her eyebrows raised.

"Dang, but you're infuriating!" Pres said feelingly. "Yes, I admit it, I would love to get into your pants. But believe it or not, I'd rather get into your mind first."

Could it possibly be true? Sam's friend Danny, back in Orlando, had said the same thing. But that relationship was so different—she and Danny really had been friends first. But with Pres, everything was just so flirty and sexual all the time.

Okay, Sam thought, *maybe I should give him the benefit of the doubt. Maybe I should try talking to him about something that is important to me. If he runs away, he runs away. I can live with that. All it'll mean is that I really didn't lose anything, anyway.*

"Well," Sam began, "I've been really upset, you're right." She took a deep breath and looked away from him. "I just found out that I'm adopted."

"You just found out that you're adopted?" Pres echoed.

Sam nodded her head, mute.

"Well, welcome to the club!" Pres said. "I'm adopted, too!"

Sam turned to stare at him unbelievingly. "You're—?"

"Adopted!" He said it again.

"When did your parents tell you the truth?" Sam asked. She had a million questions she wanted to ask him.

"When I was a little bitty kid," Pres said. "They read some picture book to me about how special I was because they picked me. When I got old enough to read, I read it myself."

"And how did you feel about it?" Sam asked eagerly.

"I don't rightly remember," Pres said. "Well, that's not true. I remember thinking that every time I did anything bad it must count double, on account of I was supposed to be so special and everything."

"That's just like what Ms. Miller said," Sam mused.

"Say what?" Pres asked.

"Somebody told me about kids feeling like that," Sam said. "Listen, can you imagine how you'd feel if your parents had never told you, and you just happened to find out when you were nineteen?"

"Bummed," Pres acknowledged.

"Bummed is right," Sam agreed vehemently. "I just don't know if I can ever trust them again."

"But you love them," Pres said.

"I don't even know that," Sam said softly.

"Listen, did you love them before?"

"Yes," she admitted.

"Well, they're the same people," Pres said. "They just made a mistake. Haven't you made mistakes?"

"Tons of them," Sam said with a small laugh.

Pres lay back in the sand and propped himself up on one elbow. "From my way of lookin' at it, love is a wonderful thing to have in this world. I know plenty of people who know their birth parents, and they didn't get half the love I did."

"Yeah," Sam said softly. She thought about the Jacobs twins and their mother. Her parents had never, ever put her through anything like that. And no matter what happened, she also knew they would never stop loving her.

Pres put one finger under Sam's chin. "I understand why you feel angry, but you need to work it out so you can make your peace with them and with yourself."

"How did you get so smart?" Sam asked him.

"By bein' extra dumb for an extra long time first," Pres chuckled. He pulled Sam down and cradled her head on his chest.

"And here I thought you were just another pretty face," Sam said softly.

Pres turned slightly and gently touched the back of Sam's head, bringing their mouths together in a tender, delicious kiss.

"It's too bad you can't kiss," Sam murmured with mock sadness. "I may have to take pity on you and give you lessons."

"And homework," Pres said in a low voice, kissing Sam again.

The sunset ride back to the Jacobses' was awesomely beautiful. Sam leaned her face against Pres's back. For a moment she felt a pang of regret that she was leaving for Japan just when she was beginning to appreciate that Pres might actually be someone real in her life.

"Hey, thanks, really," Sam said when she'd gotten off and handed Pres her helmet.

"My pleasure, ma'am," Pres drawled with a twinkle in his eye.

Sam looked at him intently. "Pres, did you ever want to find your birth mother?"

"I've thought about it," he answered. "But I can't say I ever actually did anything about it. I do know there's an organization that helps people find their birth parents."

"Really?" Sam asked. A curious tingle came over her. Would she want to search for Susan Briarly and Michael Blady? What if she found them and hated them? What if they hated her? It was a scary thing to contemplate.

"I can get the name and address for you if you want," Pres said. "I've got it at home somewhere."

"Okay," Sam said. "Thanks." She was hugging Pres good-bye when Allie came out onto the front porch.

"Sam, phone call from Japan!" she screamed with excitement.

"Oh, it's Marina!" Sam cried. "I gotta run, Pres. Thanks again!"

As she ran into the house Sam heard Allie say to Pres, "I could take over where she left off." *Well, so much for her religious phase*, Sam laughed to herself.

"Marina?" Sam called into the phone. "Wow! This is so cool! I can't believe you're calling me all the way from Japan! How is it? Tell me everything!"

"Sam, it's terrible!" Marina wailed. "I'm in big trouble."

There was some static on the line, and Sam heard music and noise in the background. "What? I can hardly hear you!" Sam yelled.

"Listen to me!" Marina cried. "This whole thing is a big scam. This isn't the company my friend heard of at all. That's Show *Time*, this is Show *World*."

"Just get them to fly you home, then," Sam said.

"You don't understand!" Marina screamed. "They expect us to dance in these tiny outfits

205

on the tops of tables. They expect us to sleep with the customers!"

"Oh, God, Marina—" Sam breathed.

"I can't stay on the line long," Marina interrupted. "They won't give me a ticket back—"

"But they promised!" Sam said.

"Sam, shut up!" Marina said urgently. "I'm stuck here and I'm scared! I called Mrs. Bauersachs, but she said it really wasn't her problem—she just blew me off. I don't have anyone else to call. . . ."

"How much money do you need?" Sam asked.

"I can get a one-way ticket right away for about nine hundred dollars. Please, Sam, if you can wire it to me, I promise to pay you back every penny."

"I'll find a way," Sam promised.

"Send it to the American Express office in Kyoto," Marina said. "Thank you, Sam. I'll never forget you did this for me. I—"

But Sam never got to hear what Marina was going to say, because the line went dead.

FIFTEEN

Sam just stood there in a state of shock, trying to figure out what to do. Marina was stuck in Japan. The company was a ripoff. The dancers were expected to sleep with the customers. Marina, who rode the subways alone at five A.M., was scared.

Oh, God. This is just as much my fault as it is hers, Sam thought as she tried to figure out what to do. *I didn't even try to check out the company myself, I just believed some girl in New York named Delores whom I've never even met. How could I be so stupid?*

Sam started pacing back and forth in the hallway. *How the hell am I going to get that kind of money?* she thought wildly. Sam thought about the sad state of her bank account. She could hardly afford a ticket on the ferry, much less a plane ticket.

There was only one possibility: Emma. Emma was the only person Sam knew who was wealthy enough to pay for something like this. *But how can I ask her that?* Sam thought.

"You have to have the nerve," Sam said out loud to help her talk herself into it. "You promised Marina."

Sam took a deep breath and dialed the Hewitts' number.

"Hewitt residence," came Emma's well-bred voice.

"Hi, it's Sam," she said in a low voice. "I really need to talk with you. Do you think I could stop over?"

"Sure," Emma said. "The whole family took the ferry over to Bangor, and Kurt is driving his taxi tonight."

"Great," Sam said. "I'll be right over."

After asking permission to use Mr. Jacobs's car, Sam left immediately for the Hewitts' house, on the other side of the island. When she arrived, Emma was sitting on the front porch waiting for her.

"Hi," Emma said softly. "What's up?"

"Emma, I have to ask you the hugest favor," Sam blurted out. "I don't know what to do except just ask you."

"Go ahead," Emma said easily.

Sam sat next to her. "Okay. Here it is." She related the phone call she'd just received from Marina. "She doesn't have anywhere else to turn," she finished.

"No parents?" Emma asked.

"She's an orphan," Sam replied. "Look, I know you must want to say 'I told you so.' She and I were both so stupid! But if you can just do this for me—for my friend—I'll pay you back every cent," she vowed.

"Why can't Marina pay me back?" Emma asked.

"She could, I guess," Sam agreed. "But I'm the one who's asking you because of our friendship, so I figure it should be my butt on the line."

Emma smiled softly at Sam. "I'll do it," she said simply.

Sam jumped up. "You will? Just like that?"

"Yep," Emma said.

Sam threw her arms around Emma, practically knocking her over. "You are one hell of a friend."

"And you are one large friend," Emma said, righting herself. "I think the travel agency in town should still be open. Let's go wire the ticket to her now."

"I can't imagine what it's like," Sam mused as they got into the Hewitt's BMW, "to be able to spend any amount of money for anything you want."

"Well, it's not quite like that," Emma said with a laugh, backing the car out of the driveway.

"Just about," Sam muttered.

"So I guess this means you're not going to Japan," Emma said a minute or so later as she stopped at a light.

"Right," Sam said. Suddenly a horrible thought struck her. "You don't suppose that Mr. Jacobs has already hired my replacement, do you?"

"Are you kidding? Do you have any idea how hard it is to get a decent au pair after the season's started?"

At least I still have a job, Sam thought thankfully. Then she said aloud, "When I think of how close I came to getting stuck over there with Marina . . ." She shuddered and stared out her window, seeing the nightmare her life could have been at that very moment.

And then another thought hit her. *What if I had gone over there, and what if I didn't happen to have one very rich friend?* Sam knew she would have called her parents. Her parents, who struggled to pay the mortgage and buy clothes for all of them and put food on the table. Her parents, who had so many times gone without something so that she or Ruth Ann could go on a school trip or have special lessons.

And somehow her parents would have found the money to bring her home.

"What are you thinking about?" Emma asked as she parked the car.

"Parents," Sam said quietly.

"How's it going with yours?"

"Badly," Sam said truthfully. "What they did still really, really hurts."

"I understand," Emma said.

They walked a few doors down to the travel agency. Fifteen minutes later, Emma had wired a prepaid ticket to Marina.

"I can't believe how easily you did that," Sam marveled.

"The miracles of the modern age," Emma said lightly as they walked back to the car.

"Should we set up a payment plan now?" Sam asked.

"When Marina gets back to the States, have her call me," Emma said as she steered the car back toward the Hewitts'.

"Are you sure?" Sam asked. "Because I meant what I—"

"I know you did," Emma interrupted. "It's okay."

211

Sam looked at Emma's profile as she drove. "You're a really, really good friend, Em."

"So are you, Sam."

When Sam got back to the Jacobses', the house was completely quiet. Everyone was out.

Sam stumbled up to her room and threw herself down on her bed, kicking off her cowboy boots. She could scarcely believe how emotionally and physically exhausting the last few days of her life had been.

So . . . I won't be dancing in Japan after all, Sam thought as she stared at the ceiling. It was funny, but she didn't feel nearly as bummed out about it as she thought she would. The way things had worked out, she would have a chance to spend the whole summer with her two best friends, and to really take some time to figure out what she wanted to do with her life. Just because Emma and Carrie had everything planned out, it didn't mean she had to. *And maybe, just maybe*, Sam thought, *someday I'll get up the nerve to search for the woman and man who gave me away*. That would come later, much later, though. She had all the time in the world.

But there was one thing she had to do that

couldn't wait. Sam knew that now. She got up and padded into the hallway. She picked up the phone and called a number she knew by heart.

"Hello?"

"Hi, Mom," Sam said softly. "It's me."

THE EXCITING NEW SERIES
by Cherie Bennett

Emma, Sam, and Carrie are different in every way. When they spend the summer working as au pairs on a resort island, they quickly become allies in adventure!

SUNSET ISLAND
0 863 69800 X/£3.50

Emma, Carrie, and Sam set out for a fantastic summer of fun and independence on Sunset Island. The three get jobs working for terrific families, and the guys on the island are cuter than *any* at home. This is definitely a summer none of them will forget!

SUNSET KISS
0 863 69805 0/£3.50

Carrie's decided that this is it – the summer she finally shakes off her boring "girl-next-door" image in order to win the boy of her dreams. But when she sneaks out on the children she's caring for and gets caught by the police in a very compromising position, she discovers that boring may not be so bad after all!

SUNSET DREAMS
0 863 69810 7/£3.50

Sam thinks she's got what it takes to be a successful model, so when a photographer agrees with her, she's in seventh heaven. He wants her to go away with him for the weekend. It's up to her friends to stop her – before she makes the biggest mistake of her life!

SUNSET FAREWELL
0 863 69815 8/£3.50

Emma just can't believe what is going on right underneath her nose! It seems Diana, her worst enemy, is back on Sunset Island, and she's gone beyond being snotty and rude. She's gone after Emma's boyfriend, Kurt. But Kurt thinks Diana's great and Emma's *too* touchy ...

SUNSET REUNION

0 863 69820 4/£3.50

Sam lands a job as a dancer, Emma's turning over a new leaf and Carrie manages to get backstage passes to one of the hottest concerts of the year. Soon, they find themselves to be the centre of attention when they're invited to hang out on rock star Graham Perry's yacht. Thrown into an adult world, all three friends have to make big decisions about who they want to be.

SUNSET SECRETS

0 863 69801 8/£3.50

It's winter, and Carrie, Emma and Sam are on the road to Sunset Island for a mega pre-season party. Everyone's going to be there, including Kurt and Billy. But their journey is not without problems. And what is everyone going to think when the girls turn up with their new admirers in tow?

SUNSET HEAT

0 863 69806 9/£3.50

Sam is hired by a talent scout to dance in a show in Japan. Unfortunately, Emma and Carrie don't share her enthusiasm. No one really knows if this is on the up and up, especially after her fiasco with the shifty photographer last summer. But Sam is determined to go despite her friends . . .

SUNSET PROMISES

September 1994/0 863 69876 X/£3.50

Carrie receives a lot of attention when she shows her photos at the Sunset Gallery. She is approached by a publisher who wants her to do a book of pictures of the island. But when Carrie photos the entire island, she discovers a part of Sunset Island that tourists never see . . .

SUNSET SCANDAL

October 1994/0 863 69881 6/£3.50

Emma has started to see Kurt again, and everything's going great . . . until Kurt is arrested as the suspect in a rash of robberies! He has no alibi, and things look pretty bad. Then, Emma befriends a new girl on the island who might be able to help prove Kurt's innocence.

SUNSET WHISPERS

November 1994/0 863 69812 3/£3.50

Sam is shocked to find out she is adopted. She's never needed her friends more than when her birth mother comes to Sunset Island to meet her. And to add to the chaos, Sam and Emma, along with the rest of the girls on the island, are auditioning to be back-up in the rock band *Flirting with Danger*.

To order any of the **Sunset Island** books, please enclose a cheque or postal order made payable to **Virgin Publishing Ltd**, to the value of the books you have ordered plus postage and packing costs as follows:

> UK and BFBO – 70p for the first book, 50p for the second book, and 30p for each subsequent book to a maximum of £3.00;
> Overseas (including Republic of Ireland) – £2.00 for the first book, £1.00 for the second book, and 50p for each subsequent book.

Send to: **Cash Sales, Virgin Publishing Ltd, 332 Ladbroke Grove, London W10 5AH**

If you would prefer to pay by VISA or ACCESS/ MASTERCARD, please write your card number here.

_____

expiry date_____

Please allow up to 28 days for delivery

Name_____

Address_____

_____Post Code_____